The Boathouse Murders

Although some places, spaces, and towns in The Boathouse Murders *are real, the characters and most locations are a product of the author's vivid imagination. Any resemblance to persons living or dead is purely coincidental.*

August 2020
Montreal, Canada

Second Edition

Copyright © by David Mark Gosselin

Dedicated to:

Stanislas Olivier Gosselin

Prologue

1969, Lake Massawippi

A well-dressed older man wearing a captain's hat guides his Chris Craft through a boathouse door and into its berth. His passenger, a young woman in her late thirties, sits in the passenger seat with a lavender scarf around her head and sunglasses perched on her perfect nose. The motorboat's gunwale rubs up against bumpers, and the man cuts the motor. She refuses the man's extended hand and steps onto the platform between the two berths. He mutters that he'll join her at the cottage in a few minutes and secures the boat with nylon cord.

     Half an hour later, the man lies lifeless like a rag doll in the bottom of the boat with an ugly gash over his left temple, a chip on his front tooth, and a crooked smile on his face.

Chapter I

The builders erected the mansion in a clearing on a hill that overlooked the lake. Gothic, Italianate, bracketed and ornamental, it featured a large cupola with red bricks fired in turn of the century Eastern Township's kilns. The wrap-around veranda featured bone-white railings with spindles in perfect alignment, like a human spine.

The tenth anniversary Murder Mystery Retreat weekend would be unforgettable, according to the organizers. The script, the characters, and the facilities had been prepped with painstaking effort. The promoters further guaranteed the lakeside setting would provide an "ethereal morning fog on its motionless surface, with the surrounding woods splattering the mountainside with blood-red foliage."

Professor Bevyn Jones grabbed a seat looking down on a sunken garden. A few grey hairs grew at his temples, contrasting with his black hair. He stood about six feet tall with broad shoulders and a trim torso. His deep blue eyes were unnerving in their brilliance.

He perused the participants and crew for the individual most likely responsible. Most of the guests stared straight ahead, zoned out, except for one old woman who slept and some Gen Ys who were paired to their wireless devices, oblivious to anything or anyone else.

A murder weekend hostess dressed like an airline stewardess approached the microphone. Her jewellery and teeth gleamed in the light, while silverware clinked against fine porcelain. She had a breezy, smug manner and a voice with a slight touch of condescension.

"Ladies and gentlemen, welcome to the Bakerstreet mansion's Mystery Retreat Weekend."

The guests, mostly Montrealers and a few Torontonians, applauded, welcoming the murder and mayhem the weekend promised. The speaker continued to schmooze the guests. "I understand the rain delayed most of your arrivals last night, but I'm *so* glad to see most of you made it. Give yourselves a round of applause, please."

The guests responded with tepid clapping as they assessed one another with furtive glances in the event a neighbour or colleague might be in attendance.

"Most of you have already received your instruction packages in the mail. Remember, the individual who solves the crime receives a *free* vacation to England, the land of Sherlock Holmes, *and* $10,000 spending money! Do your best! We'll *so* be watching."

The applause level increased a number of decibels and echoed across the green lawn. A few guests fidgeted, unaccustomed to open air and seats without upholstery.

"I hope you all know your identity and have your costumes. I understand that we have with us this weekend some really great sleuths." She stuck a digit in a dimple and continued. "There's Sherlock Holmes, Ellery Queen, Miss Marple, Hercule Poirot, etcetera, etcetera. You'll be meeting them *so* soon, along with other notable and not so notable people." She flashed an efficient smile. "Does anyone have a question?"

An old man stood up, his face flushed, and waved his cane. "When does this bloody thing start?" He paused for some unknown reason perhaps a seed trapped under his dentures and plopped down in a huff.

"*Soon*," the professional woman cooed like a dove. The participants shifted in their seats, the synthetic material of the cushions making a rippling sound. "You have until Sunday at noon to guess the murderer or murderers."

As the rep fielded questions of concern about insects, water-borne diseases, as well as ticks, from the urban dwellers, Bevyn slipped away and headed down to the boathouse. Dew still clung to the grass in spots, wetting the tips of his shoes. The sun felt warm on his face, and he relished it. He sought out warm spots like a cat and enjoyed the outdoors lifestyle.

The sounds of the Q&A session faded as Bevyn neared the water. He saw the boathouse and veered to his left. Huge gaps existed between the dilapidated structure's vertical planks, and the roof ridge was bowed like an old horse's back. The wood had the weathered patina common to farm buildings in the area. The door was ajar.

As he approached the building, he heard a car, distant at first and then becoming louder and louder. A police car with a swirling dash-mounted flasher rounded the corner. A standard-issue unmarked Chevrolet cruiser came to a halt. The doors flew open, and two officers dashed over to Bevyn.

"Are you the waterfront supervisor?" the older officer asked.

"I am part of the retreat weekend."

Chief Inspector Murphy stood about five feet ten inches tall and always wore an Expos baseball cap. No one but his ex-wife knew if he had any hair. Pipe tobacco stained his irregular teeth. He spoke French with grammar and an accent that would send tempers soaring at the *Office québécois de la langue française*. Detective Roy was smallish and had a scar on his chin he denied his first wife inflicted.

Murphy levelled his eyes at Bevyn like a bobcat, ready to pounce. He scratched his chin. "Why don't you tell us what you know?"

"I got here about five seconds ago."

The elderly cop put his hands to his hips, and Roy brushed his holster. Bevyn intuitively let both of his hands drop to his sides.

"I was invited to the weekend. I received an email early this morning to come here. I have no idea why."

Murphy muttered under his breath. "Where's the super?"

Bevyn shrugged. "I didn't see anyone. Like I said, I just got here when I heard you two coming."

Murphy nodded to Roy, who went and cordoned off the area with yellow tape and then ran into the boathouse. Roy came back a few seconds later.

"White female. Blow to head. Terrible."

Murphy's eyes swept over the area again. He spotted a man dressed in a suit approaching them. He wore a name tag on a lanyard around his neck with the Bakerstreet mansion Mystery Retreat Weekend logo. The man squared his shoulders and sized up the older cop. "We own this boathouse. What seems to be the trouble?"

Chief Murphy returned the favour by giving the officious man the once over. "That'd be me, but take a number." He pointed in Roy's direction. "Talk to him." The official balked, and Roy uttered an expletive.

Murphy focused his attention on Bevyn. "What's your name?"

"Jones, Bevyn Jones."

"Chief Murphy."

The men shook hands.

"What did you see when you arrived?"

Bevyn waved his hand. "Nothing unusual, except the door to the boathouse was open."

Murphy grunted. "Stay where you are."

He edged over to the boathouse and peered inside. His eyes took a few seconds to adjust to the dim light. The building smelled of rot, two-cycle engine oil, and canned tuna. Old fishing tackle, life preservers, rusty cans, and licence plates cluttered the floor in one corner. A cardboard advertising poster hung on the wall. It illustrated a young teenage couple from the '50s marvelling at a cola in the boy's hands.

A nude female body lay in a rowboat that rocked in the water like a cradle. Murphy's face hardened. He grunted and edged back over to Bevyn just as Roy finished with the rep. Roy waved his notebook. "The rep says super don't answer eez phone. He go check him."

Roy's words hung in the moist lake air along with some mosquitoes. Murphy gave Roy a grimace and twiddled his fingers for the detective to spill everything.

"Da man say he know nutting. He says he having hard time keeping persons at mansion."

Murphy scratched the back of his head, a habit he had picked up from his father. "Go throw a blanket on the body, but be careful not to destroy any evidence. Then go find the super."

Roy went to the cop car, retrieved a blanket from the trunk, and carried it to the boathouse. A few curious retreat participants started to gather. Roy left the scene and ran up the lawn toward the mansion.

Bevyn clarified the series of events with the chief. "I received a text early this morning." He peered at the boathouse door. "We were supposed to meet here."

Murphy levelled a gaze at the university professor. He put his hands on his hips. "Why you?" The chief tilted his head to one side, like a stroke victim.

Bevyn pointed at his Sherlock Holmes costume as a possible explanation. Murphy pinched his nose with his fingers. "What did this email say?"

"Come to the boathouse at 8:00." He showed the chief the email on his cell.

Chief Murphy shook his head in dismay. He motioned to the dilapidated structure and was about to say something when a siren blared in the distance. A few seconds later, a marked car from the provincial police arrived on the scene, and two uniformed officers rolled out. Murphy yelled an expletive and burst into staccato franglais, a mix of French and English. The cops shook their heads in bewilderment.

Murphy pointed at each cop in turn and then the surroundings, giving orders. "You, check outside this building, and you, keep an eye on the crowd." They hesitated, unsure of Murphy's orders. But after a few seconds of deliberation, they followed them.

Murphy went into the boathouse, leaving Bevyn at the door. He removed his sunglasses and waited a few seconds for his eyes to adjust to the gloom before stepping into the boat. Avoiding the blanketed body, he removed a flashlight from his pocket and looked inside the boat.

Bevyn was waiting outside when two guests dressed in flannel shirts, suspenders, and Shur-Gain caps approached. They wanted access to the crime scene, thinking the spectacle was part of the weekend. Bevyn stood his ground and told the two keeners a police officer was inside investigating. Murphy heard the commotion and came to the door.

"What's going on out here?"

"We're here to investigate. See, we have special privileges," the younger of the two men boasted, pointing at a special pass hanging from a lanyard around his neck.

"This is a crime scene. Back to shovelling manure."

The other man pounded his chest. "We're just playing the game. We got a right to access." The man's sidekick just blinked, unsure of what to make of the police officer's comment.

Bevyn shook his head over the absurdity of the situation. It was unintentional parody in its finest form. The chief glowered at the two men until they beat a hasty retreat, vowing to take up matters with the management.

Murphy slapped Bevyn on the back. "Thanks for that, Jones. Whatever *that* was."

The chief went back inside the boathouse and swept the flashlight's beam inside and outside the boat until he spotted something in the water. Murphy knelt and retrieved the item. It was a faded black-and-white photo. He flipped it over. The back had date on it.

After checking the body and the rest of the boathouse one more time, Murphy joined Bevyn outside. The chief showed the professor the picture and waited while he studied the image. Bevyn shook his head, unable to identify the picture of a young woman sitting on a car fender. The retired cop produced a plastic envelope. "It may be a picture of our vic. Did the person indicate a name in the email?"

"Ladybug," Bevyn muttered under his breath.

Murphy shrugged his shoulders and dropped the photograph in the envelope. Detective Roy appeared out of the crowd. Though breathless, words tumbled out of his mouth. "We find super in his room. Hit on head. Can't talk. *Tabernac*! More people coming. Everyone tinks eez a party!"

The chief swirled saliva around his mouth. "When we start hauling them in, they'll wake up."

"Do you think that's wise?" Bevyn wrapped his knuckles on the door jamb, a plan hatching in his mind as he spoke.

Murphy let out a sarcastic, guttural laugh, and Roy rattled off, "Nous ne sommes pas *idiots, Jones!*"

Bevyn raised his eyebrows and replied in a British accent worthy of Sherlock Holmes, "Chaps, once they know, what's going to keep them from leaving the retreat?"

Roy stared at Bevyn with his eyes narrowed. "*La loi.*"

The chief choked on his saliva and then shook his head. "Okay, humour us. What's your plan there, Sherlock?"

Amidst Roy's bellyaching about police procedure and punctuating the end of Bevyn's sentences with French profanity, the professor presented a plan. At the end of his monologue, Murphy's body language belied unspoken assent. Bevyn celebrated with a snap of his fingers. "Let's make it count!"

Later at the mansion, Bevyn sat in a large living room that had been converted into a contemporary/retro eatery. In one corner was a large dark-stained Adam-style cupboard, detailed with carved pilasters and cornices on top and rosettes and fans on the lower doors. The floor looked original and was polished to a high gloss. Each entrance had pocket doors, and two sets of antique lights with oblong bulbs hung from the ceiling. At the far end, French doors opened to a small terrace, where a few guests sipped cups of tea and mugs of coffee and espresso.

Bevyn placed his glasses on his head and reached for his hot beverage of choice: rooibos. He sipped the South African red tea, wondering about the request to meet at the boathouse. He reached into his breast pocket and extracted his cell. The action did little to distract him from his annoyance over the article in the official mystery retreat newsletter *Sleuth* lying on the table. A large headline announced, 'Murder in the Boathouse' with an accompanying article.

> *According to the police, around 7:00 a.m., the waterfront supervisor found the body of a woman in the boathouse. The woman has yet to be identified, but her skull definitely*

received a blow from a large blunt object. Foul play is suspected. All guests are asked to read their clue packets.

He felt uneasy about the article's transparency, but the opportunity to use his deductive skills to get to the bottom of the young woman's death propelled him forward. Most locals knew he taught English literature at the local university and that he liked to solve puzzles. But he hadn't expected to be involved in a real murder.

He examined the people seated around the room. Sitting nearby were two young women, obviously Torontonians judging by their reserved manner and Valley Girl banter. The brunette had a nice oval face, and her blonde friend had her hair up with a few strands dangling down around her ears in ringlets. The former had the sculpted face of a prom queen, and the latter looked like a younger version of an actress on one of those perpetual adolescent television sitcoms.

Detective Roy approached Bevyn from behind. Bevyn maintained his composure. Roy pulled out a notebook with one hand and a pencil out of thin air from the other like a magician. He waved it in a circle as he eyed the stained-glass windows with a fleur-de-lys motif above the door.

"I check you out. You from around here," Roy said.

The Quebecois had a manner about him that intrigued Bevyn, who liked offbeat characters. Roy scribbled a few notes in the notebook he always carried with him. He wrote hastily, like his life depended on it. Noises escaped from his throat as he assessed Bevyn through some internal dialogue.

"You like to solve crimes?" Roy said.

"Why do you ask, detective?"

Roy fiddled with the pencil and scanned the room. He let out an exclamation of unknown origin. "You tell me."

"I am here to help, Roy," Bevyn answered in French.

Roy calculated his next move. The computation complete, staccato words tumbled out of his mouth. "Da boathouse make news before. Some guy slip and bang eez head."

Bevyn's eyes drifted to an old man seated in a corner, dressed for a safari. He tapped his head as if he was flicking on a switch leading to his brain's memory centre. "A body in the boathouse . . . local businessman, John Peters. He and the original owner of the mansion, Arthur Engleside, were involved in an investment scheme together. The investigation determined it was an accidental death."

"No proof of dat." Roy pulled on his lower lip while motioning with his head at the other guests in the room. "Get many invitations to deese tings?"

"I try to filter them out."

Roy frowned. "See woman over dare?" Bevyn followed the French Canadian's gesture as the officer pointed with his pencil. "He's an actor on TV, a *téléroman*. Dis case will be very hard."

"Tell me. Get anything on the photo? I'm trying to remember where I saw it."

"Meet the chief in place of supervisor in fifteen minutes." Roy trotted off, placing the pencil behind his ear.

Bevyn spotted a woman entering the room. She wore riding gear, complete with black boots and a riding crop. She stood about five feet ten inches tall and moved her body with a mixture of femininity and athleticism that Bevyn found compelling. As she passed Bevyn's table, he caught her eye.

"Lost your mount, Miss . . . ?"

"Scarlett," the woman responded with a touch of mockery in her voice.

Bevyn let out a loud chuckle. "In the billiard room with a pistol?"

"That's the old game. Now it's the spa room. And you would be?"

"Guess?"

She played with her hair and let her eyes travel over Bevyn's costume. "Sherlock Holmes. Elementary." She folded her arms across her chest. "Wait a minute. Where's Watson?"

"Funny thing. They didn't give me one." Bevyn noticed her eyes, bright, alert, and dark green with gold flecks.

"Curious that they gave you a Sherlock Holmes getup," she said with a smile as she adjusted her blouse. Scarlett studied his profile, noting the hardness of the jaw line and the softness around the eyes. She brought her eyes to his, which had been occupied in places that she found amusing. "You find anything interesting?"

"No, just keeping an eye on that crop." The way she held

her chin reminded him of a painting of a woman by a French Impressionist he had seen at the Met in New York City.

"Oh, this. I find it attracts far too much attention."

Scarlett rolled her head around and ran her hand sensually down the nape of her neck.

"Last night was such a blur. So much rain on the roads, I thought we'd be flooded out."

The tussle in his mind became fiercer as a dormant mix of drives and emotions awakened. He heard the sound of the espresso machine hissing as the barista prepared a cappuccino.

"When did you get here?"

"Around 10:00 last night."

"Alone?"

She wriggled her ski-jump nose. "Ha! Wouldn't you like to know!" She studied his face. "Good thing the waterfront super found the body."

Bevyn imagined how her soft white cheek would feel under his fingers. He had forgotten about the softness of a woman's skin, the tickle created when two pairs of lips brushed one another or at a flick of an eyelash on the cheek. . . .

He cleared his mind. "Yes, he certainly was Johnny on the spot." He removed his smart phone from his lapel pocket and checked the time. He made a curt, salutary wave with a hand and departed before the woman could say anything more.

Asking directions on the way, Bevyn found the waterfront supervisor's room on the third floor. He peered in. The place looked like a cyclone had swept through it: tables, chairs, books, and paper littered the floor. Most telling of all, a young man with a bandage around his head stood in the middle of the room stood. His hands were in his pockets, and he leaned back on his heels. The definitive developmentally arrested late thirty-something, he wore cargo pants and an anodised purple karabiner hung from his webbed belt. Streaks of maximum hold gel coated his hair.

Bevyn entered the room just as the super let loose an outburst of shock and amazement. "This is so effin' gnarly!"

Chapter II

Chief Murphy heard the supervisor's exclamation and came out of a back room just as Roy arrived at the apartment door. Murphy recalled his experiences with new bosses and gave the detective a thumb up. He needed the Roy's support or things would be difficult. Already, the detective showed some attitude, and Murphy didn't know if it was due to language, recalcitrance, or both.

The chief acknowledged Bevyn with a curt nod. Roy gave his superior a brief sidelong glance, while the man-child was eyeballing the three older men with scorn.

"My head hurts, eh?" the super said.

Roy ignored the remark and took a quick glimpse around the room's perimeter.

Murphy offered the super a compassionate gesture with his hands. "Sorry, but you're our new best friend."

Bevyn bent and picked up a piece of letter-sized paper, reversed it, and brought it to a window. He pored over it with the scrutiny of a scientist. Roy gave the professor a quizzical expression.

"Looks like a boot mark. A very big boot. Some toe wear, heel worn at thirty degrees," Bevyn remarked. He directed a question at the super who was sitting in a chair near the door. "What's your shoe size?"

"Shoe size, Um, ah, nine and a half. Why?"

Bevyn eyed the super's feet and stared at the imprint. "Just wondering." He handed the paper to the Roy. "Looks like a size twelve hiking boot. High end, Zamberlan or Scarpa."

Roy took the paper and stared at it like it was a printout of his elevated Prostate-Specific Antigen level test. The janitor arrived on the scene. The devastation elevated his blood pressure; he fumed. "I want to know when I can start cleaning up."

Murphy exclaimed that the room would be ready soon and waved the man away. The janitor left, muttering to himself. Roy fiddled with the paper. Murphy snatched it away.

"By the wear, I'd say we're looking at a tall man who walks pigeon-toed," Bevyn added.

Murphy's jaw dropped, and Roy scrunched up his face like he had indigestion. Ignoring them, Bevyn cleared his throat. "Do you mind if I have a go with the super?"

Murphy shook the paper. "First tell us about the boot, Jones."

"The heel wear is typical of tall men, and you can figure out the toes yourself. Surely, you've studied footprints?"

"They didn't teach us that in police school," Murphy said, scratching his head.

Roy erupted in caustic laughter. Bevyn repeated his request, and Murphy assented. Roy let out a note of protest, but Murphy gave the tempestuous detective his back.

Bevyn sidled over to the super and smiled. "Tell us what happened this morning."

"I regularly check up on things, eh? I do maintenance too."

Bevyn took off his hat and slid the rim round and round in his hands. The waterfront supervisor maximised total obliviousness, as if he were at the end of a video game, waiting for the next to load. "Your name is?"

"Clint."

"As in—"

"Yep."

The super heard Roy's loud snort and rolled his head. He let out his breath. "She's dead, eh?"

"Very."

He tossed back his head. "Reminds me of the video game *Killer Instinct*. Ever play?"

Bevyn stopped twirling the hat and tried a different tack. "You called at what time?"

Clint raised his eyes to the ceiling and rolled up the shirtsleeve on his right arm. "I dialled 911 right away, but the phone didn't work. Figures, right? Just when you need the effin' thing, dead zones around the Townships kick in. Huh, dead zones. Frig! How ironic is that? Anyway, I come back here, and my place is totally wrecked. So I call anyway, and, like, as soon as I put the receiver down, *boom*! Out of nowhere, someone clobbers me. Why wait until I call? Man! I thought the babe was an inflatable doll or something, you know? But then I saw the blood. Frig, I told the French dork, eh? Don't you guys talk?"

Roy grunted and took a step toward the super. Murphy barked. Roy stopped in his tracks and snapped the pencil in his hand in two.

Bevyn examined the super's face for a few seconds. "Who found you?"

"Oh, the maid. She saw the door open."

"How was the body lying in the boat?"

Clint looked at Bevyn's clothes. "Are you for real?"

Murphy came over and spoke in a more authoritative tone of voice. "Just answer the question."

"I dunno, like a rag doll. Well, no, not really. Tidy, face down, arms at her sides like a dead body, you know? Like on TV, eh?"

Roy snickered and Clint's nose twitched. Bevyn noticed a tattoo on the man's arm for the first time—a door hinge at the joint between the upper arm and the forearm.

Murphy cleared his throat. "Did you see anything else? Anything suspicious?"

Clint, undaunted by Detective Roy and enjoying the spotlight, made a hip-hop move with his hands and gave a negative. Murphy was about to let the super go when the young man tapped his head.

"I saw a Rottweiler. He was pissing on the fountain."

Bevyn frowned and opened his eyes wide. "So, they have guard dogs around?"

"Well, no. That's the funny thing, because of the guests and all. I mean, when there isn't anyone, it's totally chill. But with the weekend, forget it."

The janitor dropped in for another visit, and Murphy ignored him again. He stomped off in a huff. "What do you make of the Rottie?"

"I know one of the boss's men has one."

"What else?"

The super adjusted the bandage around his head. "My head hurts. I can't remember anything else. I'm leaving."

The chief squeezed the young man's shoulder. "You've had quite a morning. Best take it easy. Let us know when your head clears. It's vitally important." He motioned for Bevyn to follow him to the hallway and instructed Roy to stay with Clint.

Bevyn pointed at the paper in Murphy's hand and proclaimed. "He's hiding something."

"You think he's involved?" Murphy asked.

"Who knows?"

The chief pulled a handkerchief out of his pocket and blew his nose. Bevyn liked the chief's old-school style. "Did you show him the picture of the dead lady?"

Murphy nodded in the affirmative. "He said she was one of the retreat participants."

The two men didn't talk for a few seconds. Bevyn asked the chief if he could do some investigating of his own. The corners of Murphy's lips ratcheted up a little, and he shrugged. "Just stay away from Roy. He thinks you're a nut job."

Murphy slipped the paper into an envelope he produced from his jacket, brushed his nose with his first finger, pointed the digit at Bevyn, and went back to the crime scene like a bloodhound on the trail of a fugitive.

Bevyn followed a long corridor lined with lithographs of the Eastern Townships. The hallway ended at a gooseneck wall lamp with an art-glass shade and a stairway leading down to a fire exit. He hoped a walk along the shoreline would clear his mind.

Once outside, he joined the guests milling about the

grounds. Most of the guests were in costume, while others were dressed in more contemporary clothing, taking liberties with the program. The lawn felt soft underfoot, mossy and green. Crosshatch patterns of sunlight danced on the surface of the water. An old man approached him from across the lawn. He was fitted in a suit jacket with black pants and a bowler hat.

The man chuckled at Bevyn's costume. "Dressed as Sherlock Holmes, eh? Whatever are you doing here?" The man's eyes narrowed as Bevyn extended his hand and introduced himself. The man took the professor's firm handshake. "Lawrence Holt, communal capitalist."

Bevyn inquired as to the origin of the man's title and got an earful about the need to give capitalism a gentler, human face. Bevyn made an offhand remark about corporate greed, whitewashing and false humility which was met with a glare. They talked briefly about the weather and generalities about the retreat weekend until the senior brought up the death of the woman in the boathouse.

"So very sad. I hate these things for that. Tend to romanticize murder and crime."

"So why do you come?" Bevyn asked.

Holt was taken aback by the professor's question. He avoided it and true to his contradictory nature, commented on the obvious instead, throwing out a hand and gesticulating with his fingers toward the lake. "The motorboat out there's making a hell of a racket. What the hell do they need all that power for?"

Bevyn had heard the sound of a boat with a rumbling 50-hp outboard motor searching the lake around the boathouse for clues. He steered the conversation in that direction. "Maybe you've seen something out of the ordinary?"

The old man drew his hand to his forehead to shield his eyes from the sun. One of his eyes wandered, and the pupil did not dilate—a glass eye. "I expect you mean anything about the murder. No. I almost solved the murder last time around." The man pursed his lips. "I'm afraid my wife drags me to these affairs."

Bevyn saw a patrol car pull into the drive. An officer jumped out and hastened to the mansion. Bevyn excused himself and tipped his hat on his way to intercept the officer. He caught her at the door. "What's the big hurry?"

She grabbed the door handle and pulled in one fluid motion. She gave Bevyn a quick once over. "Talk to Murphy."

"We got a lead about the picture we retrieved from the water?"

The officer ignored him and entered. Bevyn followed her from a distance into the former Engleside Mansion. The officer went straight to Murphy and discreetly handed him an envelope. Murphy took a quick look as Bevyn approached him.

Murphy announced the arrival of the deceased's family. Bevyn inquired about the envelope. Chief Murphy tapped his shoe by way of a response. He stuck a finger between his neck and shirt collar and ran his finger around it. "I hate doing this."

"Me too, but we've got to focus on the big picture," Bevyn said.

"What happens when they find out, Sherlock. What then?"

Before Bevyn had a chance to press the chief further about the contents of the envelope, an elderly man wearing a large overcoat that reached almost to his knees entered the room. He combed his grey hair straight back and wore a pair of reading glasses on the tip of his nose. He supported his wife, a woman in her seventies with iron-grey hair, watery eyes, and a large mole on her chin. The granddaughter trudged close behind. She was young and so slight; Bevyn thought she might blow away in a strong wind.

The chief quickly ushered them into an adjoining room. He gave them the rundown of the situation and expressed his sympathies. He hoped it didn't sound too pithy.

The words didn't register with the mother and girl, but the man nodded politely. He produced a recent picture that showed a young woman in her late thirties with a pretty face and larges eyes. In the photo, her head was tilted, and she appeared vibrant and smiling.

"Who took it?" Murphy asked.

"Her boyfriend," replied the granddaughter.

A ladybug flew into the circle and landed on the girl's arm. She shook it off. Mrs. Samuels kept a tissue in her hand and dabbed her eyes from time to time. "Did she suffer?"

Roy brought his hands together. "Blow to head. Boom, boom."

Mrs. Samuels burst into tears. The chief glared at Roy and tried to smooth over the detective's lack of sensitivity. After a minute he asked, "Did she have any enemies?"

The three sat in silence shaking their heads. "What about the boyfriend? What's his name?"

"Robert? Pleasant enough fellow. He's an engineer. Wears one of those iron rings on his finger," Mrs. Samuels exclaimed.

The chief laid a hand on Mrs. Samuels's shoulder, arose, and moved out of listening range. Bevyn and Roy followed. The three huddled in a corner.

"Locate the boyfriend," Murphy instructed Roy. "And get copies of that picture out, ASAP. We've got to struggle through this awful quagmire . . ."

The detective opened his mouth to speak, thought better of it, took the picture from Murphy, and left. Murphy rejoined the family, leaving Bevyn standing alone.

Bevyn lingered, checking his cell phone for messages. As he finished checking his inbox, the family exited the room looking bewildered. No one had asked to see the body which was strange.

A shadow fell across Bevyn's smart phone screen. He felt lightness in his chest, like his insides were being tickled by a feather. He didn't look up. "What's up, Scarlett?"

"What's up with you?" She tossed her hair back. "Hey! How did you know it was me?"

Bevyn focused on the spot between her lovely eyebrows. "I pick up vibrations people emanate."

She erupted in laughter, snorting loudly through her nose. She prodded him further. "Was it my perfume?"

Bevyn stared her straight in the eyes and almost drowned. "I have my ways of knowing. In your case, it's not too hard. You move a certain way."

Her face soured at first and then she grinned over the implication of Bevyn's observation.

"Sorry about earlier. I had a matter to attend to as a man in demand," he offered by way of apology. He put away his phone to give the woman his full attention.

"I think I may have something," she whispered and pulled him into the library by his coat sleeve. They stood at the only door to the room. She let her shoulders drop in an exasperated huff.

"Aren't you curious about how I found out about the murder?"

Bevyn opened his eyes wide. "No."

"You're Professor Bevyn Jones."

He spread his hands in ignorance. "I'm just playing a role."

"And the police chief is just playing a role, too?"

He tweaked his body posture, feigning wounded pride. "What's your name?"

She spoke between gleaming white teeth. He noticed for the first time that one of her incisors was a bit smaller than the other.

"Jennifer Watson. I'm right, I know. I took one of your courses on Poe at the university."

"I remember you. You're a big fan, right?"

Jennifer rolled her eyes. "I enjoyed the readings and your lectures on crime fiction."

"Glad to hear, but . . ."

"You don't remember me, do you?"

Bevyn adjusted the sleeves on his coat, ignoring her comment, and steered the conversation back to the main thread in an attempt to maintain a professional distance. "What do you have for me?"

"Gotcha! Back to work. So, I walk into the dining room, and the next thing I see is a man and a woman together. Such a cliché, right? Anyway." She took a big intake of breath. "He's dressed as the Count of Monte Cristo or something. They dance for a while, but, suddenly, I see her push him away, and she takes off, with him in pursuit."

His eyes wandered to the large and dark furnishings in the room: country Hepplewhite chairs, a buffet with ornate brass escutcheon plates, and a high style Sheraton sideboard with finely turned reed legs and serpentine front.

"So far, it sounds pretty tame to me."

Jennifer, unfazed by the professor's comment, continued her story. "Off they go into the night. It could have been her."

"What do you mean?"

"Well, the woman looked like a friend I had in college. Caroline."

"Caroline?" Bevyn remarked and blinked.

She nodded. He brought his eyes to the part atop her head.

"You cannot say for sure?"

"Tough to say. Normally, I'm good at faces."

"What about the guy?"

"Tall, late thirties, black hair, crooked teeth, and very small wrists."

Jennifer flinched when a voice filled the room. "Can I get you folks a drink?" A server leaned between them like a stage actor on cue. He had a California tan, bleached hair and big, beefy biceps.

Bevyn scanned the room, bewildered. "How did you get in here?"

"It's a secret. My name's Victor. Can I get you a drink? I know I could use one."

"Do you always sneak up on people like that?"

Victor lifted his nose in the air and eyed Bevyn with contempt. "Not usually. I tried to make some noise, but you folks were so intense." He switched demeanour. "We have a special drink today called 'Styles Affair.' It named after an Agatha Christie novel. It's mango and pomegranate with rum."

"Ah, no thanks," Bevyn replied. He described the woman and man to the server.

Victor tapped his lips with his first finger. "She was totally rude, treated me like the hired help. But really, you got to wonder about people who come to these kinds of things. No offence, but murder for fun? There must be something Freudian to it."

Bevyn and Jennifer exchanged glances. Bevyn apologized for his gruffness and repeated the description. "Do you think it's her, Victor?"

The server nodded his head. "I served the *bi-atch* a drink."

"No companion?"

"Some guy in a cape like Batman. Hideous costume."

"Would you recognize him?"

"He wore a half-mask just like the caped crusader. Hard to tell. I'd recognize his voice, though. He had a mouth on him like a drunken sailor." Victor corralled a few dishes on a settee behind them.

"Anything else you remember?"

"Are you kidding me? She wore some Goth thing with a horrendous neckline. She even complained to me about it." Victor retrieved the remaining glassware in the library. "I don't know about you, but this is all very sexual to me. There's talk the body in the boathouse was found naked." He shook his head and brought his hand to his hips, waiting for confirmation that wasn't forthcoming before exiting in a huff.

Bevyn tapped his fingers on his chin. "Did anything else happen in the garden?"

"Ah, no. Nothing like *that*. They didn't stay long. I think they heard me. What is it, Bevyn?"

"I dunno, but I'm going to find out." He tipped his hat. "My room number is 113. Keep me posted." He slipped away, and Jennifer followed. He reached the foyer and stopped. Jennifer banged into him.

"What are you doing?"

"Sherlock needs a Watson, and I am Jennifer *Watson*."

He saw a dancing flame in her pupils that radiated passion and vitality. As Bevyn considered Jennifer's offer, she spotted a man out of the corner of her eye and pointed in his direction. "That's the guy!"

Before they knew it, the caped man darted away and fled down the corridor, pushing through the crowd of guests and staff. Bevyn anticipated the man's destination and made for the front door. The man changed direction and headed for the parlour. Bevyn plowed through a crowd, cutting across the room. The man saw an open window. He made it about halfway through when his cape caught on a nail protruding from the window ledge.

Bevyn seized the cape. "Going somewhere?"

The men struggled until Bevyn succeeded in pulling the suspect back inside. Bevyn shoved the man into a chair. He sat sullen, stroking his jaw. "What do you want?"

"Why did you run?"

The man examined Bevyn's frame. "Let me effin' go." He yelled. "Someone get the cops! This guy's nuts!"

Roy entered the room and threw his hand in the air. "Jones! *Tabernac!*" He rushed forward, horrified by the situation.

Jennifer explained what had transpired in French. Roy's face screwed up. "I take care of it."

Roy asked the caped man to follow. He arose and, in a flash, ran toward freedom. Bevyn stuck his foot out, and the man went flying, landing at the feet of a growing crowd of spectators.

Roy picked him up and sat him back down. He reached into the man's lapel. The man grabbed the detective by the wrist to stop him. There was a struggle until Roy pinned the man's arms behind his back. He motioned to Jennifer who reached inside the man's jacket and produced a wallet. She showed the driver's license to Roy.

"What's the name of da woman you were with last night, Mr. Brent?" Roy asked.

"Brent's my first name. I have no idea. She said she was Betty."

"I saw you two together," Jennifer interjected.

The man struggled under Roy's grip until Bevyn whispered in his ear. "Why were you running?"

The man rotated his head and gritted his teeth. "Screw you!"

"You guys were arguing," Jennifer remarked.

"Just a little acting, you know? I'm Oscar material." The man ogled Jennifer, licking his lips as if savouring every inch of her body. "We experienced great carnality, eh?"

Bevyn blew a piece of lint off the man's cape, so deliberately and lightly it was intrusive. The onlookers began to talk about the unfolding drama, starting a buzz that swept through the mansion.

Roy lifted the man up by his hands. "Let's go outside."

"I can't wait," Brent said, curling up one side of his mouth like a snarling dog.

They reached a slate terrace overlooking manicured lawns bounded by flower beds of blue and white hydrangeas. A helicopter flew by overhead. Roy released Brent's hands and picked a quiet, uninhabited spot to drop the bomb.

"You lady friend eez very dead, *monsieur*."

The man gaped. "What? Impossible!" His jaw muscles tightened as he realized the situation he was in. "We had a drink and then she left. That's it!"

"*Tabernac*," the detective cried and brought his face within centimeters of the man's. Brent snapped his head back.

"She wore a lot of war paint. Hard to say. Who'd want to kill her?"

"When did she leave?" Jennifer asked.

"Late, like midnight or thereabouts. We had a great time."

Roy clenched his fists. Brent sidled over to the balustrade and rubbed his hands together. Bevyn rolled his shoulders and peered at the suspect with suspicion.

"You have drink, and you not know if eez her. What she wear? You remember dat?"

Brent glared at the detective and spit into the bushes. "She was alive the last time I saw her. Now, leave me friggin' alone!"

He hurried down the steps and crossed the lawn. Bevyn and Roy moved to pursue, but Jennifer stopped them in their tracks with a loud voice. "He won't go far."

Bevyn wheeled around while Roy remained rooted to the spot. Bevyn gave her an incredulous stare. "How do you know that?"

She held up a wallet and waved it in the air like a flag. "Because he forgot this."

Brent reached the edge of the lawn and disappeared into the surrounding woods. Roy stomped off muttering to himself, and Bevyn and Jennifer stared at each other, considering the ramifications of Brent and the dead woman's tryst, no doubt just one among many at Bakerstreet. Bevyn examined Brent's wallet further and wondered about the man's motives for attending the weekend.

Chapter III

Bevyn's smart phone beeped at 1:00 p.m., reminding him how many hours had passed since the events at the waterfront. The coroner placed the time of death around midnight. The morgue photo of the victim's face and shoulders revealed a pretty face—a life, a promise squashed. Bevyn didn't like the police practice of showing morgue photos to suspects, even though he knew a reaction, body twitch, or eye flicker might expose the culprit and save time and effort.

    He turned on the faucet. The pressure dipped and then water shot out, soaking the front of his pants. To make matters worse, someone knocked loudly at the door, he received a text message, and the house phone rang, all in quick succession. He froze for a second debating what to do, when the person at the door knocked louder. He picked up the house phone and shouted into the receiver for the caller to wait.

    He covered the mouthpiece and shouted at the person on the other side of the door. "Who is it?" He heard Jennifer's muffled reply.

He looked at his wet khakis. "Just a sec." He grabbed a robe lying on the bed and threw it on. He dropped the phone on the floor and opened the door to an empty hallway. He hustled back to the phone.

"Next time, lover boy."
"Whaddya want, Roy?"
"Murphy want to talk."
"Tell him I'll be by later." He hung up and read the text on his smart phone:

```
Ladybug has a hard shell
```

Bevyn drove to Sherbrooke in a nostalgic mood. He passed through the graffiti spattered and tattered downtown core with its late 19th-early 20th century collection of buildings, including the art deco styled Granada Theater. The area had not changed much since the days when policemen directed traffic at the King intersection in a "garbage can," a round enclosure painted black with yellow caution stripes.

He had mixed emotions about returning to the area. Had the tenure position not materialized he would not have returned. His friends were in the city and he liked his position at McGill. But the area's mountains and lakes and the city's pollution and congestion had convinced him to leave.

Bevyn arrived at the station, which was housed in a nondescript single-level glass and steel building. An officer led him to Murphy's office, and they passing curious desk cops on the way. The chief sat at a creaky old oak chair, pouring over evidence. The pictures of the body had a few coffee stains on them, and the corners curled upward. He covered up the pictures with a newspaper. Roy popped into the office; he eyed the visitor with unveiled suspicion and contempt.

"Get back to finding other suspects, detective," Murphy ordered. He went back to reading the super's statement as Roy shuffled off, returning to his desk. The chief pushed a pastry into his mouth and winced.

"Got a cavity?"
He waved his hand in the air. "Just a sensitive tooth."
"Anything on the pic in the water?"

The chief shook his head and put a coffee cup to his lips, swishing the contents around his mouth like mouthwash. An officer tapped on the door with a fax, dropped it on the desk, and left.

"Whaddya know. Can't find an address. The last known we got is her parents in TO. That's not all." Murphy pressed on his tooth through his cheek. "We located the ex-boyfriend. We're bringing him in for questioning."

Bevyn nodded and silence fell between them until Murphy broke it. "What's it like in Wales?"

The professor's face broke into a grin. The chief responded with a knowing smile. "A few phone calls were all it took."

Bevyn scratched his chin. "My grandfather hails from a village near Snowdonia and Harlech Castle. I went back to visit a few years ago. It's a place of rolling hills, and you're never far from the ocean."

Murphy grunted. "I enjoyed being near the ocean out in Victoria. Supposed to be my retirement home after a life of serving and protecting."

He slid the file across the desk. Bevyn picked it up and leafed through its yellowed contents. He tweaked his earlobe as he read. The ceiling fan spun off-kilter overhead. "Why did you give me this?"

"I want you to tell me what you know."

Murphy's smart phone rang, and he pulled it out of his pocket. He listened and hung up after a few grunts. He winked at Bevyn. "It'll have to wait. Williams just arrived."

The sun slipped through a seam in the cloudy horizon, blazed across the sky, shot through the dirty police department window, and hit the retina of an average man in his late thirties. Williams had brown hair and eyes, a small mouth, and signs of premature balding.

"Hey, that light's blinding me," the suspect protested.

"*Bonjour, mon ami*. You like to hit women?"

"I don't know what you're talking about."

"Ha! You know nutting."

Murphy stood with his hands on his hips, holster jutting out, gun butt inches from the suspect's face. "Mr. Williams, what can you tell us about Caroline?"

"She's my ex-girlfriend. What's this all about?"

Roy leaned over the table, blocking the light. "*Very* ex . . ."

Williams leaned back as if nauseated by Roy's aftershave.

"As in very dead," Roy proclaimed with more emphasis, like an exasperated babysitter talking to a rebellious tot.

Williams's face went white, and he loosened the collar of his buttoned-down shirt.

"When did you see her last?" Murphy asked.

Williams ran his hand through his hair, removed his glasses, and rubbed them on his shirt. "Been a while. I had to put some distance between us since the breakup. I can't believe it."

"She dump your ass?" Roy baited the man.

"No, it's not like that."

"You hear of new guy and *boom, boom*?" Roy clapped his hands together.

"Ah, no. New guy? *Really*?" Williams removed his hands from the table and placed them in his lap. "I broke it off with her, for your information."

Roy sat down and faced Williams. He stared into the man's eyes. "Why you break off?"

"She was always busy, you know? 'Let's go to the movies,' I'd say. 'Too busy,' she'd answer. Or I'd suggest we get outta town, and she'd tell me 'I'm busy.' I had to make an appointment to see her, almost. You know, the modern woman."

"And dat make you very angry."

Williams' manner turned peevish. "No, she just liked industriousness. She was always was happy to see me, almost like my dog."

Roy screwed up his face and almost spit in the corner. "Someone following her?"

"A stalker, you mean? She never said anything."

Williams sat stone-faced and held his hand up to block the sun again. Murphy shook his head at Roy. The detective arose, and he and the chief exited the room. The experienced police officer motioned at the suspect with a tilt of his head. "We're wasting time."

Roy opened his mouth to speak, but Murphy silenced him with a pre-emptive grunt. "Find some new angle, a friend, a student, anything. Find out what she was into, who she confided in."

"And the boyfriend, Chief?"

"Let him walk his dog."

An officer entered and handed the chief a report. Murphy read it and shook it like a thermometer.

"What is it, Chief?"

"More autopsy findings. Our lady is . . . was . . . pregnant."

After the brief interrogation, Bevyn and Murphy re-entered the office and sat in comical seriousness with the door ajar. Murphy was muttering under his breath about the behaviour of modern man while Bevyn studied the victim's report. He put the report down. He felt like a voyeur. He wondered if maybe that was the whole hook for him: a way to connect emotionally to people in a controlled manner. It bothered him that he had trouble forming bonds with people because his brain was always working on overdrive.

"The examiner found scars on her wrists. A few years old," Murphy remarked.

The professor took a deep breath. "Suicide attempt?"

"No, the examiner doesn't think so. Not deep enough. Probably signs of cutting. First I've heard of it. You?"

"It's usually linked to poor self-esteem as a result of abuse and neglect."

Bevyn watched the chief digest the information with discomfort. He tossed the pictures back in the folder and shook his head like he was trying to dry his hair.

The older man stifled a yawn, closed the file, and leaned back in his chair. "You okay?" Murphy said.

"That's one dead with an innocent child in the mix. I don't like it one bit."

The chief nodded. "We're running her DNA to find out if Williams might be the father."

A slight breeze moved the curtains in the office window, and a fly flew erratically over the chief's desk. Murphy caught it out of thin air, arose, and released it out the window. "Life's precious. We gotta find the bastard who did this."

Murphy recalled the case of Josephine Lynch, an office

worker who was found dead in her apartment downtown. The autopsy determined that she had been strangled to death. She, too, had been pregnant. They focused on the boyfriend right away, but he'd had a rock-solid alibi. The case remained unsolved, a cold case nagging at the policeman like a sore thumb. Murphy had made a vow that it would never happen again, not on his watch.

Bevyn told him about the text message.

"We'll check it out. You think it's the same person that drew you to the boathouse?"

Bevyn grunted. The chief drummed on his desk with his fingers. "Roy's going to go over the boathouse again with the proverbial fine-toothed comb."

The professor supported the plan and changed the subject. "Brent seems all talk."

Murphy assented. "Roy filled me in."

The chief studied Bevyn's face with the eye of a trained psychologist. "It was your idea to play this one out."

"It'll pan out. What about the family and the body?"

"They haven't said a word yet, and I don't know why."

The two men sat staring at each other for a few seconds. Bevyn broke the silence.

"Anyway, about the file on the first boathouse death, I can't add much. The victim had lots of coin. He profited from his businesses. Rumour had it that he lived a double life. Among the suspects at the time, his wife, business associates, and the servants at Engleside Mansion—which the place had been called before it changed hands—the family lawyer stood out, but the detectives on the case couldn't establish motive, other than a business deal gone wrong. There was talk of a mistress whacking him, but no evidence."

The sun slipped behind the afternoon clouds and they fell silent, each caught up with the implications as the dying light filled the squad room. Bevyn cleared his throat. "I figured I'd bring you up to speed."

Murphy waved his hand in the air to quash Bevyn's embarrassment. "I asked earlier, remember?" Murphy placed his thumbs in his suspenders.

"Yes, yes. Anyway, the detectives on the case called it an accident, saying that an inebriated old guy slipped and banged his head while going for a midnight cruise," Bevyn said.

"With a mistress . . ."

"That's the rumour," Bevyn replied.

The chief leaned forward, hanging on Bevyn's words. "What do you think, Sherlock?"

"I don't like to speculate without evidence."

"It's all there in the file. They just couldn't put it together back then. Human nature hasn't changed much since Cain and Abel. I like the mistress for it." He took a deep breath.

It disturbed Bevyn that nothing much changed under the sun: all that time in school learning to make a better world where science and technology would make everything better and human beings stop killing each other, only to reach a New Millennium where it could be done more efficiently and in greater numbers.

"I do think there's a link between then and now. Maybe we caught a break."

"Two birds with one stone?" Murphy said.

Bevyn arose to take a closer look at a poster on the office wall with the Chinese character for "courage" on it. After studying the image for a few seconds, he proclaimed, "And lightning rarely strikes twice in the same place."

Locals snickered over affluent city people paying for murder. After all, the city was chock full of individuals knocking each other off. Why did they need to come to the country for more? As if to answer the question, the well-heeled guests at the mystery retreat escaped further into denial, eager participants in a lie that they could not control.

Guests obtained motives and clues at the front desk with Bakerstreet "currency." In other words, the show went on. The organizers hinted at possible suspects and encouraged everyone to think "outside the box" to find the murderer. *Sleuth* called the weekend "a celebration of all things murderous."

Bevyn found a path behind the mansion that wound through the thick forest. The clouds that had brought late-morning showers had moved eastward, and the sun appeared. He picked his way along the path for a few minutes until he saw a familiar face heading in his direction.

Lawrence Holt peered at Bevyn with his one eye while the

glass eye stared straight ahead. He approached, peering at Bevyn with curiosity and faint recognition. "My knees creak like trees and I can't find my teeth!"

Bevyn stifled the urge to laugh. He spotted a crust of toast on Holt's shirt pocket accompanied by a smidge of peanut butter. "I'm up at the weekend retreat, doing sleuthing duties. We talked this morning."

The man peered closer at Bevyn. "Too long ago. What did we talk about?"

Bevyn moved a leaf on the ground with the toe of his left boot. "We talked about murder retreat weekends and if you knew anything about the murder."

The old man nodded as his synapses fired. "Good luck with that one!" He studied the other visitor's face and waited for Bevyn's response. The man saw something in the professor's face and lost a bit of his crispness. Bevyn prodded the ground again.

The old geezer erupted. "People today are raised on too much damn television! They can't separate fantasy from reality. I'd look into the first death in that damn boathouse. A man just falling and hitting his head like that . . . After all, he was a rich man." He saluted and brushed past Bevyn and continued on his way along the trail, weaving from side to side. Bevyn watched him go and resisted the temptation to pursue him for further details.

Bevyn reached the end of the path where he found a fire pit and some benches. A slapdash wooden cross sat on an even cruder altar that overlooked the lake. A steep cliff dropped down to the water behind it. Bevyn peered over. He liked heights and saw a gull circling below. He heard the crack of twigs and whirled around. He scanned the woods and cocked his ear, but there were only a few wrens moving about and strips of birch bark flapping in the wind.

Bevyn jumped when an object whistled through the tree branches. He dove for cover under the altar. Something hit the altar with a thud and stuck. He waited, breathing hard. He heard a female voice in the distance. It echoed through the woods. He peeked out from under the altar, but could not see his assailant.

Minutes earlier, Jennifer had decided to take a walk in the woods. She had dressed in her most fetching pants and a short sleeve top.

After a few minutes of tramping on the trail, she had heard a commotion ahead and seen birds scattering.

She spotted Bevyn walking toward her, sweat on his brow. "Hullo, there!"

"You show up at the oddest times. Was that you calling?"

Jennifer nodded. "You look horrible!"

"Thanks! Someone thought I'd look good mounted on a wall." Bevyn's chest heaved as he recounted the close call.

"Are you okay?"

"Just a little rattled."

He removed an arrow from his pocket and rubbed his jaw. He noticed the tiny mole for the first time on Jennifer's lower cheek. "Crossbow bolts with little chance of prints."

Bevyn stopped. It struck him how natural it felt to have her by his side—which made things more complicated. Modern amateur sleuths worked alone.

Jennifer smacked her lips. "Bevyn, the waterfront super takes pictures of the guests as they come in."

Bevyn hesitated only a second, distracted by the close shave in the woods. He grasped her inference. "So, there's a connection between the pictures and the trashed room?"

Jennifer gave a sly smile. "The person or persons who trashed the room were looking for Clint's digital camera"

Bevyn made the connection. "You mean—"

"Clint's camera was stolen."

"How do you know?"

"I did some detective work on my own. I am good at this kind of thing." She winked at him. "Also, I wonder about the series of events. For instance, why did the suspect wait until after he called 911 to bop him?"

Bevyn's face went slack, and he opened his mouth to speak, but Jennifer interrupted him. "Anyway, he saved the pictures to his laptop. I asked him to forward them to me via email."

Pine needles created a soft carpet underfoot as they walked. He could have used more fresh air, but he knew the pictures couldn't wait. As they approached the mansion, they sized up the impressive façade made of blocks of limestone and regular stone quarried from a mine near the Vermont border.

They entered the mansion's stone walls seconds later to a

sea of guests dashing around, hot on the trail of a murderer. After reaching Bevyn's room, they sat side by side, the blue light from the LED screen reflecting off their pupils.

"This kid's sure thorough. Every picture has a caption with the name of the guest," Bevyn remarked.

Jennifer scanned the hotel manifest as Bevyn scrolled through digital images. He called a name, and she checked it off. A text on his smart phone announced a new message. He clicked on it.

"Crap."

"What's up?"

"I keep getting texts."

"What kind?"

He closed put down the phone and called out another name. "Never mind, I'll tell you later. Charles Lemoyne?"

"Check."

"Brigitte Black?"

"Check."

"James Bower?"

Jennifer uttered a strange sound with her mouth. "There's no James Bower."

"What about Shawna Ball? They arrived together."

Jennifer reached over Bevyn's shoulder, touching his arm as she double-checked the screen. They both received an electric shock but continued in professional decorum.

"We have a mystery couple."

"Dressed as Bonnie and Clyde, it appears," Bevyn observed.

They finished the list and then re-examined the photo. Bevyn printed a few copies. He gritted his teeth and threw back his shoulders. He tried his best firm but compassionate voice, "I don't like you involved in this."

"I already am. Are you sure this isn't just about territory? You know, Alpha dogs around a hydrant?"

He saw the next question coming and continued, "Very funny. I'll let you know, I prefer bushes. Look, I let you help me search the pictures, but this is dangerous stuff. I can't risk you getting hurt. I almost got killed out there."

"Believe me, Bevyn, I have no plans of getting hurt. I can

34

take care of myself."

He deflected the intensity of her eyes, but she continued. She shook her head, arose, and threw her bag over her shoulder before moving to the door.

"We'll find her killer. I have no doubt in my mind. I'm pretty shook up right now."

Bevyn closed the cover on the computer his mind racing. He ran his tongue along the inside of his lips.

Jennifer paused. "What is it, Bevyn?"

"You're holding back something."

"You are the one holding back."

They glared at each other until Jennifer sighed. "Let's just say it's my business. You're just an amateur." She bit her tongue, realizing the harshness of her comment and exited in shame, leaving the door wide open.

Bevy's eyes lingered on the spot where she had stood, stunned by the last comment. He pulled out his cell and examined the new message on the screen.

```
Ladybug has wings that carry her far
```

Chapter IV

Bevyn studied a painting by the American artist Wilbur Reaser who made the Township's his home and a source of inspiration for a brief period in the late 1800s and early 1900s. The portrait hung above the fireplace in the ballroom. It featured a woman reclining on a love seat, reading. The woman and Jennifer were twins. All around the professor, the urban guests milled about ingesting late afternoon finger food and cocktails as Bob, over a PA system, delivered an official Bakerstreet Mystery Retreat update.

    Bevyn spotted Jennifer interacting with people, her hair done up just like the lady in the Reaser painting. She paused now and then, keeping an eye out for suspicious activity. Roy darted about, too, but with far more obtrusiveness.

    Jones slipped out of the drawing room and headed to the third floor. He had just reached the top of the staircase when he heard a scream and the sound of shattering glass. He dashed down the corridor like a gazelle.

    When Bevyn reached the room, he saw a maid in the doorway, her face aghast. He peered inside. A woman lay splayed across the bed with a knife in her back. Drapes fluttered in the breeze from an open window to the left of the bed. The maid offered no response when Bevyn prodded her for information about the assailant. He heard footsteps pounding down the hall. Someone announced that there had been another murder.

Roy hit the scene out of nowhere, miffed. He beckoned Bevyn over and leaned into his ear. "She not dead."

"She's got a knife in her back."

"*Une pièce de théâtre.*" Roy plodded down the hall with his shoulders slumped. Bevyn stared back in the room. The woman lifted a hand, waved, and went back to playing dead.

Victor passed the door and muttered an expletive. People from downstairs bottlenecked the corridor. Bevyn heard the stomp of heavy boots on the staff staircase. Murphy burst onto the floor, and Detective Roy followed one step behind him. One glance at the professor's eyes confirmed the story, and he put his hand to his head.

"I could be doing the back nine in North Van. I want to know why we're outta the loop on this one."

"I didn't know you played," Bevyn remarked.

Murphy barked some orders at Roy, who left dispirited. They shuffled down to the end of another hallway, away from the commotion. Murphy stopped and gazed out a window at the lake, his thoughts gravitating to the cold case. "This idea of yours is a pain. I want to find this woman's killer, but, well, you know."

Bevyn took out some bubble gum and offered the older man a piece. Murphy waved his hand, declining. Bevyn popped a piece in his mouth. "I hate this as much as you, but we need an edge to find the culprit."

The chief screwed up his face. "You think it'll work all this pussy footing around?"

The retired cop reminded Bevyn of his sensei: wise, gentle, and firm, plus Murphy had street smarts to boot. The chief was a fiercer combination, admired by everyone.

"I want the killer found just as much as you do, Chief."

Murphy let out a rude sound with his lips, "We're not looking for the Massawippi Monster here."

Bevyn adjusted the cuffs on his coat. "I hear she only comes out at night. But seriously, Chief."

Detective Roy arrived with the Bakerstreet manager, Bob, and some hired gorilla called Mack. Murphy gave the two men the once over as Bevyn faded into the background. "There's a problem here, Bob. We're not communicating."

Bob tweaked his paisley tie, rolled his shoulders, and brushed the lapels on his designer suit. He was a man in his late forties with thinning hair and a nasal voice. He had a youthful face and impeccable teeth.

"I'm acting normal. Isn't that what you told me to do?"

Roy uttered the solid Quebecois expletive, *"Tabernac."*

The gorilla stepped forward, and Roy faced off with the challenger. Roy gave the gorilla a very thin smile and muttered something under his breath. The gorilla's presence was short-circuited when Murphy ordered Bob to lose the muscle. Bob assessed the two officers and then snapped his fingers. Mack swaggered off in a huff.

Murphy and Bob squared off like two rhinos in the Serengeti. The manager adjusted the buttons on his Italian dress shirt. "The guests pay for reality and that's what we give them. I'll try to keep you up to date, but that boathouse thing really messed up our plans."

"I doubt her family would call it a *thing*. Keep doing stuff like this and who knows how long we'll take." Murphy waved his hand in dismissal. Bob didn't move. Murphy smacked his lips and sauntered off with Roy. They joined Bevyn, who had gone back to the bedroom.

Murphy sought the professor's opinion. "What do you make of him?"

Bevyn struggled with some of his biases toward personality types like Bob. The man had an appearance and briskness that raised his alert levels. He responded once he was sure the manager was out of earshot. "I think he's a businessman first and a human being second."

Murphy tilted his head in agreement. He asked Bevyn to stay in touch and sauntered down the corridor with Roy. The amateur sleuth could hear their raised voices as they sparred. He took the staff stairs down to the kitchen. He pulled out his smart phone and checked the latest text message.

```
Ladybug spots are unique like
fingerprints
```

An hour later, Bevyn took a tour of the grounds surrounding Bakerstreet. He reached the tennis courts and stopped to savour a memory of his grandfather playing singles on the courts in N.D.G. in Montreal. Rich cousins had paid for the membership, and it was there that "Gramps" had met Helen Begbie, his eventual wife. He felt the air move and heard Jennifer's voice.

"I found them!" Jennifer proclaimed.

Bevyn got a whiff of her shampoo and images of springtime and lilacs danced in his head. She joined him at the fence. "There's a house next door to the mansion called Colby that they use for overflow. The Englesides lived in it for a short time after some financial problems forced them to rent out the mansion."

"Have you talked to them?"

"That's our job, isn't it?" Jennifer gave Bevyn a wink.

Bevyn tapped Jennifer on the shoulder. "Let's go over for tea."

"We'll need something better than that," she said, pressing a finger to her lips while considering possible strategies.

Jennifer raised the collar on her jacket, and they headed in the direction of the Colby House. The night air smelled of wet leaves and wood smoke. Their shoes crunched over the gravel path while bushes swayed on both sides in a gentle wind. They heard the sound of a dog barking from across the lake. It was a mournful sound, hollow like much of Jennifer's early years with her father working a lot and her mother involved in community activities.

"They have a room on the second floor, according to the manifest at the front desk," she said.

A motorboat engine coughed to life somewhere on the lake. The two-cycle engine grew louder as it approached the shoreline. The engine died, and the sound of voices carried up from the lake.

Colby House was a Victorian with red brick, white window frames, and a large porch with Roman pillars that dominated the facade. The front door was a deep red colour with stained glass windows framing the top and sides.

Bevyn knocked on the door. No one answered. He knocked

again. The voices from the lake grew louder. Bevyn motioned to take cover, and they hid behind a cedar hedge. Two men and a woman emerged over the rise, laughing. As they approached the front of the house, the two detectives recognized one of the men and the woman from the super's pictures.

James stopped and took out a cigarette and lit it. Shawna produced some keys and dangled them in her hand.

"You coming in?" Shawna said.

"You kidding? These could be the last warm days of the year."

They kissed while the stranger watched. Shawna opened the door and went into the house. The screen door banged shut. The men shifted their position. The stranger spat into the hedge, just missing Bevyn's pant leg.

"We need some kind of plan," the stranger observed.

"Look, it's perfect. We're at some dumb effin' mystery thing. What could be better than that? What are you worried about?"

"I'm not worried. You're the one that should be worried."

Shawna called to them from the screen door with an offer of food. They complied with boyish energy. Bevyn and Jennifer pondered their next move, whispering.

Leaves carried by a sudden strong gust of wind swept across the path, and somewhere across the lake, a car alarm went off. Streaks of outboard motor oil reflected off the lake. An elderly couple came down the path arm in arm and climbed the steps to the front door. They opened the door, and the mystery man exited, tipping his hat on the way out. He skipped down the steps and headed for Bakerstreet. The man stopped and lit a cigarette. Jennifer and Bevyn watched him take a few drags and then move on.

"We need to split up. You stay with Bonnie and Clyde. I'll follow the mystery guy," Bevyn said.

"I think we should stick together."

"If things get hairy, use your cell. Obviously, Colby House has many guests." Bevyn left without another word, leaving Jennifer with her hands in her pockets.

A minute later, Bevyn entered the mansion, trailing the stranger from a safe distance. He saw someone coming and resumed his normal stride. It was Victor of the hospitality crew. Bevyn grabbed him by the arm.

"See that guy up ahead. What do you know about him?"

"Some dude, nothing fancy. Pedestrian."

"Come on, Victor. You can do better than that."

Victor smiled in a conspiratorial manner. "Bad tipper, typical jerk-face, if you ask me. Some soap actor, I heard."

The servant tugged on Bevyn's sleeve. "Push on that bookcase at the end of the hall."

Bevyn spied the bookshelf and sought confirmation, but Victor had already left. He reached the bookcase and did as instructed. To his surprise, it opened, and he stepped inside. The gloom diminished as his eyes adjusted to the light. The floors had tiny pock-marks from years of use, and dust bunnies swirled around. Bevyn stifled a sneeze. Bare light bulbs hung from a low ceiling.

He followed the corridor until he found an exit door. He opened it and ended up in the pantry. He retraced his steps and heard voices about halfway back to the entrance. They got louder as he reached a certain section of the passageway. One of the voices had a thick accent.

"She came looking for me. I didn't touch her," an older man uttered in a raspy and sardonic tone of voice.

"What the hell did you tell her?" Bob demanded.

"Nothing," replied the older man.

"I don't like it."

"She's where we want her," remarked a woman in a warm, soothing tone of voice.

"Meaning?" Bob asked.

"Don't worry, darling," the woman advised.

Bevyn put his ear to the hidden door.

"What about the cops?" Bob said.

"What about them? They're doing their job," the older man advised.

"And Jones?"

"In the dark."

Bevyn found the release to the door and stepped into the parlour on cue. The woman gasped and the older man stiffened. Bob rose from his chair. He acted like he had anticipated Bevyn's arrival.

"Ah, Jones, eavesdropping again, eh? Must talk to the management about this."

Bookshelves lined the back wall, and a grandfather clock ticked in one corner. Huge oil paintings of men hunting and fishing hung on the walls just above the dark wainscoting. A fireplace filled the corner to the right in which a lazy fire burned. Two lamps stood on either end of the mantle. Their bases were made from communion cups.

"Bob, I didn't see you outside."

He missed the reference until Bevyn mimed a backhand tennis stroke.

"Oh, yes, we really must play a set. You *do* play, don't you?"

The woman crossed the room and extended her hand. She was in her late thirties, had blond hair and baby blue eyes, and wore a red dress with a plunging *décolletage*. "The great Professor Bevyn Jones. Delighted to meet you. My name is Olivia."

The older man held a tennis racket in one hand and a glass of sherry in the other. Bevyn placed him in his late fifties. He introduced himself as Reuben.

"Sherry there, Jones?" Reuben asked.

"Yes, thank you. About that tennis match, Bob. You're on."

Bevyn ignored Olivia's eyes studying his physique. She rarely blinked.

"Play much there, Jones? I wouldn't want to embarrass you."

"I've warmed up with Federer."

"Bob has quite an accurate shot," Olivia remarked.

Bevyn stepped toward the older man and requested the racket. Reuben passed it to the detective and went to pour a glass for the professor from a decanter. Olivia watched Bevyn test the tension on the strings. She stood sideways and swept a hand across her upper chest, the open back of her dress in full view.

"I'm surprised, Bevyn. . . . Can I call you Bevyn?"

"By all means."

"I am surprised you are so fit for a literature professor."

She stepped toward him. Bob stepped between them and took the racket from Bevyn's hand. He handed it back to Reuben.

"I hope you don't mind, Jones, but . . ."

"Don't be tedious," Olivia said and pouted.

"Oh, come now, Bob. Let's not spoil the party," said Reuben.

"What party? This man arrived unannounced."

"I'll take a rain check on that sherry, Reuben. Olivia, you are a memorable experience." Bevyn bowed to her, ignored Bob, and left, closing the passage door behind him. He then headed back to Colby House.

Jennifer fared a little better with Shawna and her man. Following Bevyn's instructions irritated her, but she heeded them. She stepped into the gloom of the foyer and noticed a bevelled mirror in a large piece of heavy furniture to her left. She caught a glimpse of her distorted profile in it, much to her chagrin. The floor creaked with every step. She hung in the corridor for a minute, unsure of her next move.

Jennifer heard a rustle, and a door opened upstairs. She hid from view, and a few seconds later, Shawna appeared and went out the front door. Jennifer came out of hiding in time to see her heading for the lake.

Shawna's blond pigtail flapped against her back while Jennifer followed close behind. The sound of water striking the pebbled shore ahead and the accompanying gurgles was like music. The lake had a fishy smell. The woman went to the shoreline as Jennifer crouched behind some nearby bulrushes. A few minutes later, she heard the sound of an outboard motor approaching. Shawna removed her sandals and waded into the water.

An aluminum boat came into view, guided by a man wearing a Blue Jays baseball cap and a white sweatshirt. He cut the motor and jumped out. Shawna sprang forward and wrapped her arms around his neck. He yelled something, and she released her hold. He glowered at her a few seconds before handing her an envelope. Shawna wanted a final hug, but the boater pointed the prow of the boat back toward open water. He jumped in, started the motor, and headed back across the water.

Shawna stomped back to the house, wiping back tears. Jennifer hung back in the shadows near the front door. There was a chill in the air. She rubbed her arms to keep warm. Bevyn arrived a few minutes later.

She told him about her adventures. He whispered for her to remain still and headed for the front door. Once inside, he peered around the corner and saw a man in a wing-back chair and a woman facing him. The man craned his head around the back of the chair, and the couple waved at the professor. He returned their greeting and headed up the stairs.

When he reached the landing, he heard Shawna's raised voice through the walls. The last step creaked as Bevyn stood on the landing, but the occupants were too engrossed to hear. He continued, passing a Queen Anne chair in the hallway. He reached the door and placed an ear to it. The couple had lowered their voices. Bevyn peered into the skeleton keyhole and saw an envelope on the bed.

A door opened down the hallway, and steps approached. He took a seat in the chair and cringed when a young woman bid him a good evening and went downstairs. He heard the door to the room where he heard Shawna's voice open and close. Bevyn sprang out of his seat, raced downstairs, and rejoined Jennifer outside.

"Get anything?"

"I saw the envelope on the bed. They were arguing about something, but I don't know what. Things got too hairy, so I left."

"Could you tell what was in the envelope?"

"I have a few theories."

Jennifer didn't press the matter because she had a theory of her own. They went back to the mansion. As they went, the surroundings triggered Bevyn's memory of a summer evening long ago. He could almost smell the freshly cut hay, see the strange streaks of light in the sunset horizon that locals claimed were UFOs, and hear the sound of the barn swallows singing as he sat on a rock in the middle of a pasture. He could remember it all, including the boundless hope and expectation in his soul that had long since diminished.

They would have to work backwards to find a motive and eliminate the suspects. Figuring out the former would narrow down the latter. But in the end, finding out "whodunit" and proving it would be two different things.

Chapter V

The sun flickered behind the white birches like a strobe light as Bevyn headed to his destination a kilometre from the mystery retreat. He went along a section of Quebec's *Route Verte*, an old railway bed repurposed into a bicycle path.

    He used the time to reflect on his past decision to become a monk, the early struggles, spiritual growth, and eventual disillusionment. A kind nun had told him once that the Church was like a hospital where scarred and scared people assembled to avoid treatment. How that insight helped him through many touchy situations with brothers and sisters! In the end, however, it hadn't been enough. He left the Church the way any man with integrity would leave: called away by the still, small voice of his soul to a life more in keeping with his DNA.

    He reached the monastery's main entrance below the bell tower. He pulled on the huge tarnished brass handle. Once inside, he smelled incense and a light cleaner. The *portière* or guest house keeper's face lit up when he recognized Bevyn. Though old and frail, he moved well and spoke with a heavy French accent.

"Ah, Bevyn, *comment vas-tu?*"

"*Très bien, Jean. Et vous?*"

The grey-haired man shook his hand and gesticulated as if he was describing the rotations of planets in the solar system.

"*Plus ça change, plus c'est la même chose*! We have added a sanctuary. Many years in the planning and now it's built."

"I am looking forward to seeing it."

The portière nodded. "We imported stonemasons from Germany."

"I heard. What else is new?"

"Many new novitiates. Many guests."

"Any strange goings-on?"

The old monk shook his head, mystified. "Whatever do you mean?"

"Any strange visitors?"

"Nothing unusual. Two men from overseas gave a talk about a book about treasure buried around the world. Very interesting."

"Why would they come here? Who invited them?"

"Dom Chevalier, of course. He likes such things."

They shared a few more words until some guests requiring his attention arrived. He insisted Bevyn say goodbye before leaving. Bevyn proceeded along the art deco corridor that led to the sanctuary. It featured alternating red and white ceramic floor and ceiling tiles. He passed by a statue of Mary with the Child. A tear ran down Mary's cheek.

He had almost reached the end of the long hallway when Dom Chevalier spotted him. He stood about five feet six inches tall, was of large girth, and had a bulbous face. Two small orbs peered at Bevyn from behind a thick pair of eyeglasses. He clasped and unclasped the buttons on his robe as he approached.

Dom Chevalier bowed his head. "The prodigal returns." There was a touch of mockery in his voice.

They didn't shake hands. The dom instructed Bevyn to follow him upstairs for privacy's sake. They went up three flights of stairs and along a long hallway to an office near the back of the building. Once inside, the dom pointed to a reproduction Louis XV chair covered with carvings of cherubim and angels. Bevyn sat and Dom Chevalier went to his desk.

The cathedral ceiling stretched twenty feet up and exposed beams met at the apex. Portraits of past doms and religious figures in the Order hung on the walls. A large clock on the wall ticked off the seconds. The office had all the cheer of a custodial closet.

"What is it you want?" Chevalier inquired in a monotone voice.

"I'm looking for Brother Peters."

The dom adverted Bevyn's gaze. "I'm afraid he's not up to visitors."

"It's important."

"He's not well." Dom Chevalier made an annoying clucking sound with his tongue when he spoke. The men eyed each other. During those laborious moments, Bevyn recalled Chevalier's distaste for dreamers and non-traditionalists, as well as the face-offs they had had over Christian tenets like salvation and resurrection. But it was more than disagreements about theology; it was a differing view of Christ's message. The dom saw a religious reformer. Bevyn saw a spiritual liberator.

Dom Chevalier adjusted the crease in his habit. A large cross on a chain around his neck jingled. He arose and raised a finger as if testing the wind direction. "You left us quite suddenly."

"This isn't the time to drag up the past. Forgiveness is more the order, yes?"

Outside, Bevyn could hear birds chirping. They brought his attention to the only window in the room through which he saw smoke billowing upward like a streamer from a rust-stained smokestack. It was part of a small cheese making operation. The different brands of cheese, Brie, Cheddar, Gouda, etc. were world famous. In the meadow below that stretched to the lake, apple trees were positioned in rows like pews.

"I didn't come here for confession. The police need my help solving a crime at the old Engleside mansion." Bevyn gave the dom the facts, underlining his involvement in the case. The middle-aged man drummed his fingers on his desk in deliberation.

"Why are you here instead of them?"

"My connection to the Benedictine Order implored me."

Dom Chevalier rose from his throne and smacked his lips. "Former connection." He ran his tongue around the inside of his mouth. "I'm curious as to why you chose to sever that connection."

"It has no bearing on the current matter."

"I will be the judge of that."

"Of course you will," Bevyn said under his breath.

The dom spread his hands wide, ignoring the remark. "I need to trust you again so I can help you and the police find this woman's killer. I am a reasonable man." Chevalier hitched the heavy robe higher up his torso. "I heard you left over a woman."

Bevyn felt heat rising to his face. "What of it? Aren't we called to love?" He immediately regretted his words. He knew they played into the dom's perceptions of him as a liberal and borderline libertarian, playing loose with the meaning of Christian love.

"Are you going to help or not? I must see Peters. It's vitally important."

"Let me see. You leave here, tell us nothing, and now you suddenly come back needing our help."

The dom made a "tsk-tsk" sound with his lips. Bevyn steeled himself for an impasse. Dom Chevalier curled his first finger, indicating for Bevyn to follow. They exited the room, retracing the way back to the main entrance. Air hissed between Bevyn's teeth. Just when he thought the party had ended, the dom stopped, produced a key, and unlocked the guest house.

"Go to the top of the stairs and turn left. Brother Peters' room is at the end of the infirmary. Be brief."

Without a word, he left, the edges of his habit sweeping the stone floor like a broom. Bevyn uttered a choice word under his breath, but wasted no time following the dom's directions. He found Brother Peters sitting up in bed intently reading a book. Bevyn knocked on the door frame. "Dom Chevalier told me you'd be here."

The old man with wispy white hair and sallow skin squinted at the visitor, but then his face brightened in recognition.

"Jones? Ah, *oui*, Jones!"

A coughing fit halted the man's efforts to get out of bed. Bevyn rushed to his aid. He waved his former student away, but the professor persisted until the old monk's head lay back in his pillow.

"It's a long time, *non*?"

Bevyn tilted his head in respect like the Japanese do. "*Trop long, mon ami."*

The room contained a bed, chair, desk, and window—Benedictine simplicity. Bevyn's presence elicited a glare from a lean and brooding monk who rapped on the door jamb. He whispered something unintelligible to the old monk. Brother Peters' face contorted, and he responded a few sharp words. The young brother muttered an apology and backed out of the room.

"You seem to be in fighting form."

"It's the fine cuisine."

Bevyn pulled on his earlobe and sat in a chair at the foot of the bed. The old contemplative laughed. His dentures glistened in the low light. Another hacking fit racked his slight frame. It stopped after a few seconds. Bevyn handed him a glass of water from the bedside table.

"You showed me how big the world is." Bevyn touched the man's arm.

The monk waved his hand in dismissal. "You already had outgrown this place, carnally and spiritually."

Silence ensued. They heard voices echoing down the long corridor outside the room and the elevator motor humming. The room was hot, and the air thick with religion.

"I hate to get down to business, but I need to know anything you can tell me about your brother's death." Bevyn filled the man in on the events at the mansion, omitting some details.

"You've pursued your vocation. Excellent! Unfortunately, I know little about my brother. He and I, ah, differed greatly as you can imagine in our approach to life. It caused friction and, sadly, separation. But as to his death, they ruled it accidental."

"Yes, but he had enemies, of course."

"Many! He delighted in having them. His mantra was that it was better to stand for something and be hated than to stand for nothing and have many fair-weather friends." The old man rubbed the stubble on his chin.

"Any threaten him?"

"None that I can remember."

The bells in the tower started to ring, and the monk bowed his head and closed his eyes, his lips moving. Bevyn watched him, recalling the daily routine of prayer and contemplation. He put a hand on the old man's shoulder after a minute. The monk's head rose, and he reached out a tree root of a hand and touched Bevyn. "Thank you for asking me those questions. I feel like a piece of china around here most of the time."

Bevyn chuckled. "You were most helpful." He lingered in the room with the old monk a while longer before leaving.

Five minutes later, Bevyn sat in a small chapel off the main sanctuary staring at an Eastern Orthodox icon. The smell of cardamom-laced incense and paraffin filled the room. The oak pews were stained a Band-Aid colour which Bevyn found amusing for its symbolism.

Monks drifted past opaque slit windows one by one like frames in a motion picture reel on their way to mass. He heard shuffling behind him. Peters edged toward the front of the chapel, pushing a cart.

Bevyn arose. "How did you know I'd be here?"

The monk waved his free hand dramatically and started coughing. He wheezed fighting for air until the fit stopped.

"You should return to your room immediately. Let me help you."

"Bevyn, stop. I remember something. There was a mistress, and they had a child. My brother kept it a secret."

"Tell me more."

The old man wavered and clutched the sides of the cart tighter. "He set them up in Montreal."

"What was her name?"

"Jane. The child's name was . . ." He touched his head.

Bevyn finished his sentence. "Caroline."

"How did you know?" The old monk teetered over Bevyn's interjection. Bevyn sat him down in a pew.

"Elementary, my friend."

"I heard the mother remarried. My brother kept it from his wife, although I presume she suspected. He was not a faithful man. Rich men like beautiful women and are easily tempted."

"Do you recall anything else?"

The old man raised a hand to shield his eyes from the halogen lights over the altar at the front of the chapel. "Do you think there's a link?"

"It's possible. I wouldn't rule it out."

Bevyn's old sensei shook his head, and Bevyn noticed that

the man's face had lost its colour. He offered to help him back to the infirmary, but Peters waved Bevyn off and mumbled something about Christian fortitude. Bevyn kept an eye on him until he vanished around the corner.

The smell of flowers on the altar revived the memory of an old hurt by a brother. All of a sudden, Bevyn felt claustrophobic and quickly headed to the exit. He took a wrong turn and ended up in a dark corridor that led to the kitchen. Out of the shadows emerged a hooded figure. The monk spoke in a low tone and hid his face. His breath was hot in the cool air.

"'*One that was a woman, sir; but, rest her soul, she's dead.*'"

Bevyn remained calm, completely forgetting about the unpleasant recent incident and pondered the quote from Hamlet. The figure darted ahead like a salamander and stopped, turning sideways and still hiding his face. A crucifix in the shape of an X emerged from the folds of his habit, and he spoke once more.

"'*No more be done: We should profane the service of the dead.*'"

The figure moved off in a strange, shuffling gait. Bevyn followed the figure down the corridor. The hooded man picked up his pace and darted to the right. The professor lunged, careening around the corner and slamming into the dom.

"Jones!"

"My apologies. I, er, was following someone. Did you see anyone . . . ?"

The dom brushed off his habit, tweaked his shoulders, and stood up straight. "Did I see who?"

"A strange monk just said a few words to me."

"I saw no one. What did this man say?"

"It is of no importance."

The dom raised a finger and squinted down the hallway, looking for the apparition. "You are a guest here. If—"

"It was nothing."

The dom sputtered vitriol. "Perhaps you should be leaving then!"

"One question before I leave if I may."

Dom Chevalier's eyes bulged. "What do wish to know?"

"The men you invited here to talk about hidden treasure.

Why did you invite them?"

"Are you familiar with The Secret?"

Bevyn nodded.

"Well, then. I read the book and friend of mine mentioned he knew some people who were searching for it. I arranged for them to come here. What of it?

"We met Brent. He has been searching the mansion."

"I don't know about that. The brothers enjoyed the talk very much. It's of great interest to us, after all there is talk of lost gold in Quebec too, left behind by Champlain."

His head shook like a bobble-head doll as he pivoted on his heel and departed. Bevyn made haste to the door. On his way, he met the portière. Bevyn inquired about the strange monk.

"Oh, that sounds like brother Kirk, the only Englishman in the Order, I believe."

"He quoted Shakespeare."

"Yes, that sounds like him. He used to be an actor in Stratford and was a product of the Royal Conservatory." The monk pointed to his head and looped his finger around it like he was tracing the flight path of a bee. "Some dementia, I think."

"He sounds pretty sane to me. Pretty coincidental dementia, I'd say." Bevyn tapped his head.

The guest house keeper's face took on a quizzical expression. Bevyn smiled and patted his shoulder to placate him. Jean nodded in polite acquiescence. Bevyn bowed and left as more memories of the time spent inside, safe, but his spirit sagging; Memories of transgressions and searching for peace, of trying to make sense of his life after living for so long in the shadows. Of days spent seeking love and hope again only to lose both.

The sun had risen higher in the sky. White-rimmed grey clouds lined the horizon. Cars filled the parking lot and customers ambled into the monastery store to buy cheese, applesauce, chocolate dipped blueberries, and cider. He watched them with curiosity for a while, wondering why they came: For contact with the immortal and spiritual, or simply to buy food processed by reliable producers. It was probably, like most of modern affairs, an amalgam of all three. His smart phone rang, intruding upon his thoughts.

"Jones," Murphy almost shouted with a mixture of excitement

and distress. "Better get back to the mansion. There's been another murder!"

Chapter VI

Bevyn reached the mansion by mid-afternoon. He yanked his Sherlock Holmes costume off a coat rack near the kitchen. He slipped it on and entered the cool gloom of the mansion. The guests' smiling faces contrasted the reality of the situation. He wondered what bugged him about it. Was it the entertainment value, the levity, or the blissful unawareness? Another thought crossed his mind. Maybe the guests' behaviour irked him because it reflected his own emotional detachment over the death of the young woman.

    The chief met him upstairs in the left wing in a morose mood, retirement a distant memory. Murphy attempted to reframe the thought by considering that it was probably raining on the "Wet Coast" anyway.

    A large bay window let autumnal light into an empty room. A fireplace with ceramic blue panels stood at one end, and at the other, a bevy of crime scene people swarmed like ants around a body on the floor. A man in a rumpled pair of jeans and a white shirt lay face down. Digital SLR cameras flashed and Roy stood in one corner like a court jester, yelling in his cell.

Murphy played with a piece of paper in his hands as investigators dressed in black overalls moved around the room. The chief's eyebrows came together. He addressed one of the investigators. "Anything?"

"Not much. Nothing visible except for a big tattoo of an eagle on his forearm," replied a tall officer with a gnome-like face.

"Can we turn him over?"

Two investigators rolled the body over. Bevyn gasped in recognition. "That's the guy from Colby House next door." Bevyn explained the events at the house to Murphy.

A Sûreté du Québec officer entered the room before Murphy had a chance to reply and waved the local cop over. Murphy didn't budge. The SQ officer motioned again for the older man to step outside with a sweep of his arm. Murphy put his cell to his ear instead. The officer hesitated, calculating his next move. He surveyed the scene and stamped his foot like a bull in a ring and left.

"What the hell does he want?" Murphy griped.

"A dance at the prom," said a heavyset investigator.

The chief put the phone away. "What was in the envelope, you think?"

Bevyn's head jerked upward, and he frowned. The chief gave him a sly grin. "Miss Watson called me." The professor adjusted his shoulders. "Of all—"

Detective Roy suddenly lurched into their space, looking as peevish as ever, his lips curling in a snarl. The chief wiggled his fingers at Roy to spill. "What is it?"

Roy wiped the saliva from the corner of his mouth and muttered something before launching into a tirade. "*Cirque de media*, Chief. Media get ID of dead man."

Murphy threw his head back in disgust. "How the hell?"

"It is actor Johnny Bell, they say."

Murphy squeezed his eyes shut for a second, and Bevyn, rubbing his nose remarked, "An actor or actor playing an actor?"

The chief pulled out a pill bottle from his pocket and popped a green capsule into his mouth. "Who kills an actor?"

"Maybe Jones know."

Bevyn ignored Roy's remark and pointed at the thespian's

boots. "He's wearing hiking boots. He might be the one who tapped our waterfront super on the noggin."

"*Merde!*"

"Bigfoot?" Murphy shuffled over to the open bookcase door. "Did you know about the passageways?"

Bevyn nodded. "Victor, a member of the hospitality crew, showed me an entrance downstairs."

The chief hollered at the investigators of his intention to go on a fishing expedition, and he headed through the bookcase opening with Roy. He waved to Bevyn. "I'll catch up with you later." Bevyn nodded and continued to wander around the room.

The air in the corridor smelled of dust, mildew, and kerosene as they shuffled along. Cobwebs hung in the corners of the aged and genuine 2X4 framing. Roy flicked on a switch, and a bare bulb glowed farther down the passageway. Murphy snapped on a LED flashlight and studied the floor. "Footprints leaving the scene."

The gloom enshrouded them like fog. They followed the passageway as it zigzagged. When they reached a descending spiral stairway, Murphy stopped and sent the flashlight's beam down into the darkness. "What do you think of Jones?"

Roy stared into the void, pausing to choose his words carefully. "He always near action."

The chief grunted, leaned over the railing, and sneezed. "Dig anything more up on him?"

Roy snickered. "He big shot professor. Like to study crimes, is tennis player. He knows aikido."

"What about his time with the monks?"

"Not very much, Chief. Just that he left very suddenly over differences with Dom Chevalier."

Murphy grunted and, without further hesitation, the police officers corkscrewed down the stairs. The smell of dampness increased, and soon, they heard water dripping. A metal door at the bottom opened with a screech to a small cave. It was about eight feet high and twenty feet wide. An opening straight across from the door led to daylight and open water. Murphy scanned the jagged, domed ceiling until his eyes settled on a tethered powerboat. He peered inside.

Roy stood with his hands on his hips and stared at the

opening. "We go?"

Murphy scratched his head. "Go ahead. Check the shoreline near Colby House. Jones and Watson identified some activity there. I'll get an officer down here to check this out."

Roy climbed into the boat, excitement carrying him back to his younger days with his father on Lac Saint-Jean. He started the motor and guided the craft through a narrow passage to the lake. Once he was through, the cop piloted the boat to a point about ten yards from the cliff wall. Bakerstreet came into view. Roy goosed the motor, swung the boat's prow around, and headed in the direction of a rowboat clinging to the surf near Colby House.

As soon as the keel hit the sand, Roy jumped out. He searched the other boat. It was empty save for a life preserver and an oar. The name on the prow had been rubbed out. He spotted narrow tracks from a woman's sneaker in the sand. He followed them inland. They led to Colby House.

He entered the house unobserved. He heard a couple arguing on the second floor, so he climbed the stairs quietly by putting most of his weight on the large banister.

He had just put his ear to the door when it sprang open and a Shawna stood in the doorway fuming. She screamed at Roy, asking what in the hell he was doing. Her boyfriend veered around the side of the bed headed straight for the unwelcome visitor. The detective stood his ground and an altercation occurred between the two men that left the boyfriend clutching his jaw in pain and the girlfriend cursing Roy.

He retraced his steps back to the boat a little rattled and returned to the cave a few minutes later. A lone officer combed the interior with a lantern. Roy located Murphy upstairs and reported his observations and estimations.

"The footprints lead to Colby House," Roy said with distaste.

Murphy took a deep intake of breath and beckoned Roy to spill all the details of his adventure inside. Roy studied the bruised knuckles on his right hand before recounting the tale.

Murphy's eyebrows rose, "Let me guess. She's no dumb blonde. You get nothing."

"Tsk-tsk, *monsieur le chef*. I get plenty."

Roy gave Murphy a dramatic flourish. "The woman have

passport in her pocket."

Murphy rubbed his hands together. "Despite your methods, we now know for sure what was in that envelope."

Jones and Murphy met in a quiet corner of the bistro and sat down. The waiter arrived to take their orders. Bevyn ignored the menu and asked for his customary fruit and poached egg with buckwheat pancakes. The waiter, nonplussed by the order, thanked him and scurried away.

Murphy loosened his belt buckle. "They're going to have to do some heavy lifting in the kitchen to manage *that* . . ."

Bevyn gave the chief and sardonic grin and then Murphy narrated Roy's adventures at Colby House. Bevyn interjected a few times but mostly listened. The conversation switched to Bell. Murphy leaned closer to the professor. "He had a DUI and major money problems."

Bevyn raised his eyebrows.

"Yeah, in the hundreds of thousands."

Bevyn rolled up his sleeves and pursed his lips. "He was that big?"

"Good-looking and married a rich wife who liked pretty boys."

"*She's* dead?"

The chief nodded and tried to avoid the dark humour endemic to the trade. He also recalled his own marriage and the exasperation and frustration of living and loving another human being. "Drowned a few years back. Went to court."

"Is that the case where she drowned in the backyard pool, and the hubby's alibi was that he was with his mistress?" Bevyn said.

"Pathetic, eh? The report says she had a drinking problem."

Bevyn rubbed his temples to coax his memory. "The Crown couldn't prove anything. He also had a sob story about trying to get her into rehab."

The waiter arrived with their food, so they let matters drop while they ate. After finishing, they wiped their mouths with napkins and continued where they had left off.

"So, he inherited big coin from his wife. Then what? He gambled it away?" Bevyn said.

"He claims to have lost big at the craps table and to have made poor investments because he was grieving for his dear drowned wife."

Bevyn sipped his latte. "You doubt it?"

"Her family is appealing the verdict and is apparently very pissed off."

"Enough to kill him?"

"Preliminary indicators say heart attack."

Bevyn brushed crumbs off his lap. "What about his boots?"

Murphy rocked in his seat and patted his stomach. "Large, but not a match."

Jennifer approached the table and sat down with a smirk. Bevyn glanced at his plate and her face.

She watched Bevyn's eyes. "There's word of another murder. I bet it's a real one."

Bevyn and Murphy exchanged glances.

"What did you hear?" Bevyn said.

"Some actor got bopped."

Murphy's phone rang. He listened and rose from the table. "I got to take this, sorry." He went to a corner of the room.

"What's up?" Jennifer asked.

Bevyn glanced at Murphy and out the window. "A certain situation has arisen."

"Cut the B.S."

"I'm protecting you, Jennifer."

"We've been through this before. Besides, I know something. That couple's linked to the Hells Angels. I noticed two Harley's around back. I checked arrest records in Montreal through a friend. They're from the compound outside town."

Murphy ended his call and sauntered over to the table. Jennifer captured his rapt attention.

"So, how's the actor on the floor with the bookcase?"

Murphy gave Bevyn a quizzical expression. Bevyn fiddled with his napkin on the table and cleared his throat.

"At least we know the bookcase didn't fall on him."

Jennifer reached across the table and snagged a grape from Bevyn's plate. "Think that the two murders are related?"

"That's a good question. We finally meet in person," Murphy exclaimed.

"Allow me. Chief Murphy, Jennifer Watson."

The chief beamed as he shook Jennifer's hand. Like many intelligent men, he delighted in a woman with smarts and looks.

"Delighted to meet you. You look just like Bevyn described you."

"He described me, did he?" Jennifer winked at Murphy.

A wan smile crossed Bevyn's face. "I have a gift for picking out details."

Jennifer snorted, and Murphy's attention shifted to the wall tapestry. Bevyn twirled a leftover morsel of food on his plate and told him about Jennifer's Hells Angels discovery.

"We know those two. We have the entire gang under surveillance. They have upped their game to include online gambling."

The sound of a helicopter flying overhead interrupted further conversation. A number of diners cast their eyes in the chief's direction. Murphy put up his hands in mock surrender. A plainclothes officer entered and called Murphy over. Reluctantly, he arose and bid them farewell.

Jennifer reacted swiftly once the chief was gone. "I planned to share the information with Murphy."

Bevyn bit his tongue. "Oh, sorry. I wasn't thinking."

She clucked her tongue. "So, the actor is really dead or what?"

Bevyn winced and nodded his head.

"Good to know. What do you think is going on with Shawna and her boy toys?"

Bevyn stuck his thumb in the dimple on his cheek, "Nothing good."

Chapter VII

Famous Eastern Township's landscapes by W. H. Bartlett lined the corridor walls. They featured scenes from Lake Massawippi's watery depths, to boreal forests teeming with deer, to streams flowing out of mountain crevices into rivers.

Bevyn found Bob's office on the top floor of Bakerstreet's west wing without any trouble. A bronze plaque affixed to the door read "General Manager, Robert Burton, Esq." He knocked on the reinforced door just in case and heard nothing. He unrolled a flannel cloth and selected a pick for the operation. After a few seconds, the lock tumblers rotated and made a clicking sound. The lock was successfully jimmied.

Athletic ribbons and plaques lined the walls, interspersed with pictures of Bob holding trophies. A country Sheraton dressing table stood in one corner, some caned chairs lined the office's perimeter, and a large oak desk dominated the area in front of a large bay window. Behind the desk, a telescope on a brass and teak tripod pointed toward the lake.

The office had the distinct odour of corruption, profligacy, and fudging. He heard a noise in the hallway and ducked for cover behind a curtain. Through the thick drapes he saw the door open, and Bob walked in. The manager paused for a second, looking back at the lock and scratching his head. Bevyn's heart pounded. Bob shrugged and went to the desk. He laid a file down and then retreated, closing the door after him.

Bevyn waited a few seconds before emerging. He went to the desk, opened the file, and stifled the urge to whistle as his picture fell out. Bob had done a thorough job. Other files were in the folder too: one for Roy, Murphy, and, to Bevyn's surprise, Jennifer. He spent most of his time on hers. When he finished, he went directly to Bob's laptop. He plugged in a high-speed memory stick into a USB port and booted up the unit from an initiation file. After some fiddling around with the settings, he pressed the "copy files" button. The operation finished, he left, closing the door.

In the corridor, he sensed someone's presence and whirled around. Jennifer stood with her arms crossed at the end of the hallway. A smile spread across her face. Bevyn felt like a kid caught with his hand in the cookie jar. He leaned back on his heels and stared at the ceiling, putting his hands in his pockets. Jennifer approached with the stealth of a puma.

"Is this in the official mystery retreat weekend script?" Jennifer remarked.

Bevyn ran his tongue along his teeth and smacked his lips. "Let's go somewhere more comfortable." He brushed past her.

"Leaving the scene of a crime?" Jennifer swivelled on her toes like a ballerina and followed. "Let's go to my room."

Bevyn whistled. "I thought you'd never ask."

"Don't get your hopes up."

He made a clucking sound with his mouth. "Impossible. Just delayed disappointment."

They reached her room and found it open a crack. Jennifer halted. Bevyn saw the expression on her face. He stepped forward, but she brought a finger to her lips and peered inside. He did not try to stop her. She reached inside the room, flicked on the light, and entered. A second later, she emerged.

"You sure you didn't just leave it open?"

Jennifer gave Bevyn a hard stare. He raised his hands, palms outward. "What? I had to ask."

Bevyn stepped into the room behind Jennifer. She began to verify the room's contents.

"How long have you been gone from your room?"

"All day."

"Anyone else have a key?"

"Just the staff."

Bevyn watched her. She felt his gaze on her and ignored it. They heard a knock on the door, and a woman of about fifty years of age sauntered into the room.

"*Holá!*" said the chambermaid, duster in hand.

Margarita and Jennifer began a short conversation in Spanish. After a few nods and "ums" and "aws," the woman left, rattled and vowing that the management would find the person responsible for the break-in. Bevyn studied the room's contents.

"She claims only Bob has another key. But between you and me, the locks in this place are pretty Mickey Mouse."

Bevyn jiggled the door handle. He bent down and brushed the carpet with his fingers.

"Whaddya got?"

"I dunno. Looks like some kind of powder." Bevyn scraped the powder into a small plastic bag with a jackknife blade.

"I usually remove my shoes at the door."

Bevyn felt her gaze on him. He avoided her eyes, and she cursed under her breath. "I thought so."

"What?"

"Who told you? Roy? I knew something was wrong when you let me go into the room."

"Chivalry is dead." Bevyn tried to suppress a smile.

"Here I thought you were just shy."

Bevyn rocked on his toes for a second. "This is an investigation."

"Even you have secrets, Bevyn Jones."

"I would have liked to have known. It makes me look bad." He peered out a window overlooking the parking lot.

"And that's all you care about?"

Bevyn ran his hand through his thick hair. She opened a dresser drawer and reached far in the back with her hand and removed a gun. She removed the magazine and checked the barrel.

Bevyn's gaze lingered on the gun for a second and then he went back to examining the carpet. He spotted her laptop. He went to it and examined the underside.

"Ever have this baby serviced?" Bevyn flipped the unit over.

"It's barely a year old."

"Anything important on it?"

"What do you think!?"

His eyes roamed the room, from the gun in Jennifer's hand to the colour of the nail polish on her fingernails, Candy Apple Red, the same as his best friend's '69 Javelin in high school.

Jennifer stretched her body in irritation. She opened her mouth to add something, but closed it. She snapped the gun magazine in position. "We're done here."

He stifled the urge to apologize. "And we were getting along so wonderfully." He gave the dresser a good once over and went to the door. "Thanks for the tour. I'll get back to you on the powder."

Jennifer raised her voice and slammed the dresser drawer shut. "Don't mention it, number one. Number two, I won't hold my breath."

Bevyn bolted from the room, antsy and perturbed. He raced down the corridor, his mind filled with memories of past relationships with women. He bumped into Bob mid-stride, a minute later. The manager had just finished playing tennis.

"Jones, the last person I wanted to see." Bob cocked his head to the side and released a snort so big he had to wipe his nose.

"The feeling is mutual, Bob. Have a good time chasing your balls?"

Bob laughed and swung the racket in his hand. "I only chase women, Jones. We still on for early tomorrow?"

"Wouldn't miss it."

Bob wiped his brow with the hem of his T-shirt, revealing his toned abdominal muscles "Are you sure? I wouldn't want you to sprain an ankle or something."

"Who uses that underground boat launch?"

Bob broke into laughter and slapped his knee with his hand. He leaned towards Bevyn and whispered, "Anybody can. It's no secret."

"What used to be in the room where we found the body?"

"It was used by a boarder who left two weeks ago. We sometimes rent out rooms. Is the inquisition over? I need to get to my office for an important call."

Bevyn ran his fingertips along the wallpaper. "What was the name of that person? Do you remember?"

"In the room?"

Bevyn sighed and gauged the number of sets it would take to trounce the dweeb on the tennis court.

"Stan, or something like that."

Bob rapped the wall a few times with his knuckles and bid Bevyn a good afternoon before hurrying off. Bevyn went down a dark corridor and headed for the empty room. A young provincial policeman stood at the doorway, staring at his cell. The cop stood like a statue guarding the tomb of Tutankhamen. Bevyn acknowledged the cop with a smile. Bevyn began speaking in French.

"Pretty dull, guarding an empty room in an empty wing, huh?"

The cop didn't move, his thumb idly swiping the face of his smart phone.

"Take a break. Go call your girl. I'll watch things."

"I got my orders."

"What's Gervais' number? I'll call him." Bevyn pulled out his phone. Noticing the officer's body language, he changed tack. "I understand no one is telling you guys much."

The officer loosened his serious demeanour and spoke in broken English. "What happen here? Gervais tell us shit."

"Two murders. The boathouse you know about. The second happened the other day in there. Two bodies in 24 hours."

"I see you with Murphy. He say you know karate?"

"Aikido, used only for defence. Negative energy redirected."

The officer's eyes glazed over. He fiddled with his cell and relaxed his entire body. He motioned his intention to take up Bevyn's offer. He dashed away with a big smile.

Bevyn wasted no time jimmying the lock with a pick. Within a few seconds, he was in the room, scanning for anything unusual. The secret bookcase door was back in place. Bevyn went to the windows. The afternoon light faded, and shadows stretched longer and longer every passing minute. He found nothing in the room and decided to check the passageway.

Bevyn retraced the steps taken by Roy and Murphy to the top of the stairwell leading to the cave. He cast the flashlight's beam around the area. He noticed a seam in one wall and made out the outline of a recessed door. After some minutes, his fingers found a catch, and the door opened.

Tables lined the walls, and scraps of newspaper from the late '80s littered the floor. Bevyn poked around a little more, checking out the discarded wiring and fluorescent lamp fixtures. He shut the door and returned to the hallway, just as the young cop rounded the corner whistling.

He spoke in Quebecois French. "I needed a break. The only people who come around here are the manager, Bob, and Detective Roy."

"Don't mention it."

The cop stared blankly at the professor, who smiled. "That's English for *pas de problem*."

The cop nodded and reclaimed his spot guarding the doorway. Bevyn marched off, fumbling with his smart phone, the furrows on his forehead deeper than ever. He called Murphy and brought him up to speed on the latest discovery.

"How did you get into the room?"

"The officer guarding the door let me in."

"Yeah, right. Must've been one of Gervais' men. Grow-op, you say?"

"At some time. The place ever been raided?"

"I'll check into it. Where are you?"

"Heading to the second-floor terrace to watch the sun slip below the horizon while sipping *cafe au lait*."

"God, man, time's running out."

"I need time to think."

Bevyn heard the audible sigh on the other end of the line.

"Caroline's no schoolteacher. She's a journalist, undercover."

"We figured that one out. To uncover what?"

"Her editor won't budge."

"Never mind. I can find out. Which paper?"

"The Montreal Post, and she's got a blog, whatever that is. I can barely my smart phone."

"Chief, what's her blog name?"

"Ladybug."

Bevyn came to a halt outside the terrace. His mind bounced in different directions like a ping-pong ball.

"Whaddya got, Jones?"

"I dunno. I'll let you know when I find out." Bevyn ended the call. He had just reached the door to the bistro when he heard a floorboard squeak behind him. He spun around. A petite woman of about thirty-five with dyed red hair and deep blue eyes stood in the hallway, her lips curled around a glass of a green liquid.

"Don't tell me you're Sherlock Holmes?" Her lips broke out into a grin wider than the Great Lakes.

"Elementary."

"My name is Isabelle."

He smiled, and she invited him to join her. Before Bevyn had a chance to respond, a man arrived on the scene wearing a pair of khakis and a polo top.

"She's just looking for attention," he exclaimed.

His jet-black hair and hazel eyes suggested a sportsman, but his face and hands had the distinctive pallor of someone who made regular visits to a tanning salon.

"Ivan, Mr. Holmes," Isabelle said.

The beefy man laughed and grabbed her arm, ignoring the professor. "Don't we have a date?"

Before the woman had the chance to respond, he steered her away. Isabelle looked back over her shoulder at Bevyn with a strained smile on her face. Brent entered the room with an aggressive walk and intercepted the couple. He reached out and pumped Ivan's hand and gave Isabelle the customary French *la bise*.

Bevyn mulled over the encounter before making a call to Jay, a seasoned reporter at freelance reporter. He uttered a few "ums" and "aws" for a few seconds before asking Bevyn to call him back on his cell.

"Good to hear from you. Sorry about that. You never know who's listening in these days. Yes, Caroline. She's, um, *was* good. She was researching a lot of stuff. That's all she told me. It's so *tough . . .*" He sighed.

"What about her computer?"

"There's a laptop," the reporter admitted.

"You know where?"

"I presume it was with her."

"Were you two very close?"

"She was in and out. Oh, you mean *that*? No, she, um, didn't go for my type. She preferred men who could provide some drama."

They kicked the can around for a bit longer and then Jay signed off to meet a deadline. Bevyn eyes went back and forth across the grounds. As he studied the horizon, the sun dipped behind the tops of the trees. He called the chief back.

"Get anything on Brent?"

"He's involved in a hunt for some international treasure with a partner."

"I think I know who is partner is." Bevyn told the chief about the encounter at Bakerstreet. "They gave a talk at the monastery. They're up to something," he added, and then asked about Caroline's car.

There was an expletive over the phone loud enough that Bevyn pulled his ear away.

"Roy is on that. Roy!" Murphy hollered for his detective.

Bevyn heard papers shuffling on his desk.

"There's a car registered to her name. Get back to you when we find it."

Bevyn brought a glass of water to his lips for a sip. He heard Roy cursing over the phone. The chief yelled a curt salutation and hung up.

Bevyn went over the facts of the case again. Whoever had planned the murder or murders—if they had been planned—sure had a great cover. What better place to hide than during an event where everyone is in costume and playing someone different than themselves? Moreover, what puzzled him most of all was what a washed-up actor would be doing with two Hells Angels and add the treasure hunters into the mix. What, if anything, did they have to do with the boathouse?

Bevyn went to the dining room. He spotted Ivan and Isabelle seated with his partner. He sauntered over with the premise of finishing his conversation with the woman. He reached the table and extended a hand to Ivan, knocking over a cup of coffee and spilling the contents into the man's lap. The man jumped to his feet. Brent uttered an expletive, and Isabelle stepped in front of him. Bevyn offered profuse apologies as the hospitality crew arrived and surrounded the table like an F1 pit crew.

The professor slipped away from the bedlam to examine the contents of the unknown man's wallet. After checking the ID, he dropped it surreptitiously on the floor near the table where the ruckus continued.

A few minutes later, the clock in the main foyer struck six o'clock, and the guests entered the dining room. Bob approached the microphone soon after to announce the plans for the evening. He wore consummate business attire. Mack stood in the background, scanning the crowd, his hands clasped in front of him. The muscle man tapped his earpiece and spoke into a mike.

The manager of the retreat weekend waited until most of the guests had arrived to speak. Bevyn watched each of the guests enter, hoping someone or something might stand out, but by the time Bob began his announcements, Bevyn had given up and decided to wander around the mansion. He went to the library, found a nook, and sat down in a Louis XV reproduction chair. A title on the coffee table in front of him caught his eye, so he picked it up and began reading.

Chapter VIII

Faded black and white photographs of Eastern Township's covered bridges lined the library walls. Bevyn recognized two: the Eustis bridge near an abandoned copper mine and the one on the road to Compton. He had a vague memory of the Capleton Road one that no longer existed. It had been set ablaze by local teens. Each photo captured a bygone era of slow travel and courtesy since only one car could cross a bridge at a time. To the city dwellers gathered at the mystery retreat, the photos epitomized the Townships, a place where decency and civility still thrived. But to the locals, the photos told a huge fib: Townshippers actually drove like urban madmen. Whether the roads were paved or dirt.

    Jennifer sauntered into the library with her hands stuffed into her windbreaker's pockets. She located Bevyn and managed a thin smile. They were alone.

    "I wanted to apologize for earlier, Bevyn."

    "For what?"

    She tossed her hair back and took her hands out of her pockets. "Right you are." She sat across the table from him. "What are you looking at?"

Bevyn pointed at the open book on the table. Jennifer leaned forward and tapped her lips with her fingers. "Whatcha reading?"

"It's a book about treasure buried by a publishing company in the '80s as a publicity stunt. It's a strange coincidence some treasure hunters were recently at the monastery." Bevyn told Jennifer about Brent and Ivan.

Jennifer picked up the book and flipped through it. "What about it?"

"People have been looking for it for awhile now. Some of it has been discovered. The clues are in a series of pictures in the book. The author died a few years ago and the locations died with him."

Jennifer shifted in her seat. "Interesting, but what does it have to do with Caroline?"

Bevyn swallowed hard over his companion's knack for directness. "What do you know about her?"

"She was the best. We drifted apart but reconnected recently via social media. I was looking forward to spending time with her and catching up."

"Did she say anything about what she was researching or about being here on the weekend?" He bit his tongue.

"Here? *Really*? So, that *was* her I saw! Are you saying she was here? Why didn't she tell me?"

Bevyn peered out the window, over Jennifer's shoulder. Fireflies blinked like LED headlights outside, a strange occurrence for a fall night in the Eastern Townships. "Okay, yes, she was here," Bevyn remarked.

Jennifer blinked. "What's the big secret?

The professor opened his hands, spread his fingers, and went on, choosing his words carefully. "I want to find out all I can about Caroline."

Jennifer looked out the library window. "Do you think I know something?"

"You don't exactly volunteer information."

"Look who's calling the kettle black."

Bevyn leaned back in his chair and studied the book on the table. "I'm a good guy." He grinned.

"Who picks locks and goes into sealed rooms? What did you find by the way?"

Bevyn rubbed his chin. "I found some files on Bob's desk," he replied.

Jennifer pointed at him with her first finger. "Well?"

"Files on you, Murphy, Roy, and me."

Outside, mist hovering over the lake caught Bevyn's attention. It created an atmosphere of foreboding, deepened by Halloween lurking on the calendar. Jennifer's smart phone rang. She glimpsed at the number. Jennifer replaced it in her pocket and ignored the caller.

Bob entered the library a few seconds later. He held a handkerchief to his brow. "I need your, ah, help. We found disturbing acts of vandalism in the basement."

Jennifer and Bevyn exchanged glances. Bob read the reaction in their eyes. He clapped his hands. "I'm running a business here. Murders I can handle, but a person drilling holes is sheer craziness."

"I think I may know what this is about," Bevyn remarked.

Bob wrung his hands and made a slurping sound with his tongue. He motioned for the duo to follow. He led them through a basement door and down a series of corridors and stairways, narrow and stifling.

A service elevator and one final corridor later, they arrived in a dark corner of the boiler room. A single bulb burned high above, dangling from twisted strands of wire. Bob pointed at a spot in the brick.

"There, see? Rats don't pack cordless drills."

Sure enough, there were two half-inch holes bored into the brick about two feet from the cement floor. A neat little pile of powder lay under each borehole. Jennifer knelt to investigate closer.

"Just to be certain, have you had maintenance people here recently?" Bevyn said.

Bob pulled out a personal organizer and waved it around like a magic wand. "I know everything that goes on in the building."

"Sometimes these guys just show up for unscheduled maintenance."

"Not on my watch."

"Please check your records first before we investigate further," Bevyn exclaimed.

Bob shifted on his feet and fiddled with the unit's buttons. He split his attention between the organizer and the holes.

"Nothing. You said you may know what this is about?"

Bevyn repeated what he had told Jennifer. A conversation ensued about the two men giving the talk at the monastery. After the manager expressed some anger and his concerns, Bevyn agreed to investigate further and the retreat manager left to tend to the guests. Jennifer removed a flashlight from her pocket.

Bevyn leaned forward and eyed the powder under the lamp's beam.

"Hey! That powder looks familiar, like the stuff from my room," Jennifer said.

Bevyn produced a plastic envelope and, using a jackknife, scooped up some powder and deposited it inside. He studied the area more. Most of the mortar was absent between the bricks near the floor, so he took out a flashlight and peered through each of the holes.

"Anything?" Jennifer said.

"No, looks like cement on this one, but here . . ."

"What is it?"

"I think there's a space behind."

Bevyn muttered something unintelligible. The space between them grew smaller. Jennifer's hair brushed his cheek. He coughed, and Jennifer sneezed. They stood up straight in unison like part of a comedy routine.

"A false alarm. It's just an empty space."

"Are you sure? I think I saw something," Jennifer remarked.

Bevyn adjusted the lapel on his cloak. The sound of footfalls distracted them. Roy's voice soon followed, reverberating off the iron supports and stone foundation.

They went to the bottom of the stairs and looked up. Bevyn flashed the light upward. The local cop blocked the beam with his arm and cussed. Bevyn shut off the light and offered an apology.

Roy gave the professor a dirty look and whipped out a notebook and spewed a collection of facts. "We found an abandoned car. Der were a few tings inside: *câbles de pannes*, radio, tapes, MP3 player, and a book."

"An MP3 player?" Bevyn said.

"*Oui*, music and video."

"Video of?"

"Lab check now," Roy replied, summarily disappointed.

Bevyn played with the flashlight's switch and scratched his chin with one end.

"What about the book?" Jennifer asked.

Roy looked hard at the text in front of him. Bevyn raced up the stairs and stuck out his hand. Roy handed him his notes. Bevyn read the title of the book out loud. It was the same book as the one in the mansion library.

"I've had it with this basement," Jennifer remarked and eased her way up the stairway. "We can talk upstairs somewhere quiet."

She considered what might be behind the wall and why on earth anyone like the treasure hunters would consider the mansion as a likely location for treasure. She decided she needed to research local history at the local museum.

They climbed back up to the mansion. Jennifer motioned to the end of the main foyer. A large greenhouse built in the 1960s was located at the east end of the mansion. The fragrance of the flowers and greenery reached their nostrils as they approached. Once inside, the three of them headed to a fountain at the far end, out of earshot of the guests.

Water bubbled and gurgled out of a flute at the mouth of a small bronze cherubim statue in the center of the pool. Coins covered the bottom. Fuchsias cascaded from above and hid the girders supporting the roof. The sky was laced with long streaks of orange, and the North Star twinkled low near the horizon.

Roy became agitated and talked fast. "*Monsieur Bob* pass time in Africa wit sick kid and ting called COBA."

"What's that?" Jennifer said.

"Children of Biblical Awareness, a small Christian cult around in the late '70s. What else?" Bevyn inquired.

"He marry young and divorce, no children."

Bevyn ambled around the perimeter of the fountain. "Interesting."

"Police investigated him for drug possession and DUI."

Jennifer and Bevyn exchanged glances. "Anything more?"

"Not very much. Many holidays, Mercedes."

"Anything more about his cult activity?" Bevyn asked.

"Murphy tinks you can help us dare."

Bevyn stopped. "Tell him I'll call him." He touched his lapel again and felt for the USB key. He handed it to Roy. "From Bob's computer."

Roy snatched the flash memory device out of Bevyn's hands. "I start to like you, Jones," he said and extracted his smart phone from his voluminous cargo pants and wandered off.

The two sleuths watched the coins shimmering in the water a few moments. Bevyn played with a vine climbing up the ironwork. "Bob is just too much of a knob not to be guilty of something."

"Is that your professional opinion?" Jennifer said.

"When the shoe, ah, boot, fits . . ."

Bevyn and Jennifer slipped out the rear door while a couple strolled in. The glow from a mercury lamp on a post lit their way. Jennifer drew her coat around her shoulders. They sauntered in the direction of a gazebo that stood a few yards from the mansion. A ladybug landed on Jennifer's blouse. She placed a finger in its path. It climbed aboard and stayed.

"We need to find the killer. Every minute that goes by, I feel more and more urgency," Bevyn muttered.

Jennifer watched the insect fly away. She gave her companion's coat a short tug. "We'll locate the murderer." Her voice echoed in the woods.

Bevyn took a deep inhale of breath and let it out slowly. He left a mist in the damp air. "Yes. And now, I'm going for a walk."

"I'm coming with you, Sherlock."

He suppressed a smile.

"I think better alone."

Jennifer's mirth vanished when she realized the amateur sleuth and professor was serious. Without a word, she broke away and took a path back to the mansion, boots crunching over the gravel. He watched her until she disappeared around a corner.

One solitary bat swooped down, braving the autumn air as Bevyn headed to the slate-coloured lake. He took the steep stairway down and found a log to sit on. The water left a thin line of brackish foam where it met the shoreline. He looked across the lake to the woods. The pine trees stood like priests over nature's mysterious mass.

He couldn't yet bring any kind of shape to the disparate facts. He popped a licorice candy into his mouth. It occurred to him that the threads may not be connected at all. He hated to speculate and craved more evidence. The distant eerie sound of coyotes howling broke the contemplative spell, and he decided to move on.

An hour after leaving Jennifer at the gazebo, he reached his room and found the door open and the interior trashed. The f-bomb was sprayed in green paint on the dresser mirror, and drawers and closets had been emptied and their contents tossed helter-skelter. Worst of all, his laptop was missing. He called the front desk and Murphy to report the break-in and then he went to the billiards room to wait and consider the implications.

He picked a snooker table near a window and lined up some balls. He had just decided on a cue stick when Olivia sauntered in. She wore a black dress, slightly less provocative than her earlier number, but skin tight nonetheless, leaving little to the imagination. She approached the table, swaying her hips and running her fingertips along the contours of her body.

"Sorry to hear about your intrusion."

Bevyn stared Olivia in the eye, and she held his gaze, her eyelids lazy and pupils large. Bevyn tilted his head. "Probably someone out for kicks."

Olivia ran her fingers along the felt. "Can I help you in any way?"

He laughed and shook his head while he examined the cue stick's tip. "I'll be fine, but I'll need a place for the night."

"I can arrange that," she murmured and brought her hands to her hips, examining Bevyn from head to toe. He caught a whiff of her body lotion as she moved closer. It smelled fruity and smarmy, like a persimmon lathered in coconut milk. She opened her eyes wide and brought a finger to her front teeth. "You play a little?"

"I'm pretty good at it."

"I used to play a lot," she said and dropped her head, hair

falling into her face. She brought her eyes up coyly. "I still do."

Something in the corner of the room caught her eye, and her body lost its languidness. Bevyn spotted the wireless camera near the ceiling. Her entire demeanour made a 360° turn. She assumed a wider foot stance, and the tone of her voice changed.

"Your new room's being prepared. Just go to the front desk. Call me if you need anything. We at Bakerstreet apologize for any inconvenience."

Before the professor had a chance to reply, Olivia took his hand and slipped a piece of paper with her room number on it. She gave him a furtive glance backward on the way out. Despite his best efforts, he watched her go, intoxicated.

His smart phone beeped. He stared at the latest message and grimaced.

```
Ladybugs live only 30 days
```

Murphy pulled into the driveway, one hand on the wheel, annoyed because he was missing an old episode of Joe Kenda on television. He arrived a minute later in the billiard room with dark circles under his eyes and dry lips. "Bevyn, why did you drag me out here?" He sniffed. "I do detect the smell of ladies' perfume in the air."

"Excellent work, Chief. You're hired."

"A lot of woman that one."

"Olivia seems to prefer men in uniform."

They sat down in a corner of the room away from the camera and spoke in hushed tones. He filled Bevyn in about the contents of Bob's computer downloaded to the USB key.

"The encryption buster boys cracked it. No mean feat. Bob's got a tidy sum squirrelled away in the Cayman Islands and Switzerland. Investments mostly, real estate, vineyards and stocks."

"Anything strange or out of the ordinary?"

"A list of numbers, non-indexed, arbitrary. Doesn't make much sense. Here's a printout. The boys couldn't tell the file type." He passed the printout to Bevyn. The professor passed it back with a large exhale of breath.

"Could be anything."

Murphy stuck an index finger in his ear. "We got two dead people and I'm starting to feel restless!"

"I don't like this anymore than you do. It broke my heart to see Caroline's family like that."

Bevyn reached into his pocket and showed the chief the text message. "What do you make of this? The same name as Caroline's blog."

Murphy pulled out his reading glasses and read the text on the screen. "You got some kind of admirer-slash-helper out there playing you or something?" He slipped his glasses back in his pocket. "What do you make of Caroline's history?"

"Jennifer can't add anything."

"I was afraid of that."

"Unfortunately, she only knows the college Caroline. People change." Bevyn arose suddenly and went to the table he had prepared for practice. He picked up the cue stick and broke the balls, sending three into pockets.

"What about your computer? Anything valuable?"

Bevyn gave the chief a look of disbelief.

Murphy raised his hands in the air. "Okay, okay, I had to ask. Roy filled you in on Bob?"

"Yeah, the cult involvement is strange, but I've heard stranger," Bevyn said.

"We need something soon, Jones."

Bevyn took another shot and missed the side pocket.

"I know, Chief, I know."

The case gnawed at his mind. He'd hoped to be much farther ahead with the motive, but a fog hung over the investigation like the kind Sherlock Holmes usually faced in Arthur Conan Doyle's London.

Bevyn struggled to keep his frustration and emotions at bay. He knew they could overwhelm him and short-circuit his mind very easily. He wanted the killer so much to be behind bars, but Rome was not built in a day and neither would be the case against the boathouse killer.

Chapter IX

Every now and then, Big Money from the Big City comes to the Townships with Big Plans for the area. Locals are seldom impressed by potential contributions to the GDP. Projects fail more often than not as Townshippers cannot be bought. Bakerstreet was the latest in a series of such ventures, except for the fact that locals dreamed up the idea, creative people designed it, entrepreneurs developed it, and contractors built it.

After the billiard room encounter with Olivia and time with the disgruntled Murphy, Bevyn headed to the front desk, passing a small coterie of disgruntled guests who were complaining about the handling of the mystery weekend. He reached the receptionist, a tall blonde woman in her mid-thirties who smiled as he approached.

"How can I help you, sir?"

Bevyn winced at the formality but summarized the situation. The woman, in her perfectly ironed blouse, nodded in professional commiseration and cut him short. "Olivia mentioned you would be coming."

A well-dressed couple approached the desk while they were talking. The receptionist held up a finger for Bevyn to wait. The elderly couple expressed their displeasure over the quality of their accommodations and mentioned a lawyer back home who would be calling. The receptionist maintained her composure and delivered a damage control statement which they ignored. They left tossing the phrase "sue their ass" around like it was the name of their rebellious first child.

"Sorry about that. Where were we?"

"The break-in, my room, Bevyn Jones, Olivia . . ."

"Let me call her." She picked up the phone, giving Bevyn an appraising once over. Bevyn reached over the desk and took the receiver from her and placed it on the cradle. Her name tag flashed in the light.

"How about you just give me the room?"

"I'm sorry sir, but she gave explicit instructions to call when—"

"Brenda, you're in charge, aren't you?"

Bevyn's dark blue eyes bored into hers and she began to fiddle with her hair ends. He broke into a grin, and she stood up straight and smiled back.

"I can give you a room on the third floor. It's usually reserved for . . ." She looked down. "Oh, so sorry! Here's a note from Olivia." She frowned.

"Is there a problem?"

"Olivia left instructions to put you in the pool house. Usually, only VIPs get it."

Bevyn adjusted his tie and ruffled his cloak. "How can I thank you?"

"Oh, it's part of my job."

She passed him an access card. She fiddled with the buttons on her blouse. He gave her a gentle wink and left.

He followed the directions to the pool house. It was located behind the main annex. A few people milled about the lit pool area. The structure had stucco walls with a terracotta roof and a large canvas awning that covered a bar area. Bevyn located the door around back and inserted the key into the lock. He opened the door and flicked on the light switch.

The interior featured a sunken living area with rooms off to either side in the shape of a Y. Bevyn admired the interior design and layout of the rooms. The decorator had opted for stainless steel appliances and a blue backsplash, recessed LED lighting, and lots of glass and bamboo while managing to keep it cozy and intimate.

He had just completed a tour of the place when the room's phone rang. The caller ID indicated it was the administration. He ignored it. He spotted a reproduction of a painting by Klimt on the wall. His phone rang.

"Where are you?" Murphy fairly barked.

"I was upgraded to the pool house."

"Olivia doing some damage control, I expect."

"We're getting close. The break-in is an indicator."

"It's no koinky-dink, Sherlock. I sent an officer over for protection in case they decide to return."

Bevyn protested. Murphy ignored his pleas.

"By the way, the text messages were sent from a server in Europe. What's a server? I really need to take a computer course."

"Not to worry. I'll give you a crash course next time we meet. And don't bother about the room. You won't find anything."

Murphy cleared his throat. "The New Guy in the office says we might be able to track down the sender, but it's a long shot."

"Let me know when you do." Someone rapped on the door. "Gotta go, Chief. Your man is here."

"He's already there? Wow! I'm impressed."

"Meet you tomorrow morning in the library, say 8:30?"

Chief Murphy agreed after some mumbling and grumbling about the hour and the back nine.

Bevyn heard a rustling at the door. He threw the deadbolt open and rotated the handle. His caution instinct kicked in. He stopped mid-turn, but it was too late. The door burst inward and two men wearing gas masks sprang into action. One of the attackers sprayed him in the face. Bevyn spun around and buried his face in his forearm, but the gas overpowered him. His training and discipline undermined, he tried to flee his attackers to no avail. The last thing he remembered was the familiar smell of dog.

Earlier that day, Jennifer drove down Route 143 to Stanstead. She passed the corner store where she bought what used to be called Popeye Cigarettes and Bazooka bubble gum as a kid.

The screen door was gone as was pretty much the whole building. It had been replaced by a Tim Hortons. She usually never spent much time dwelling on the past. She usually preferred to live life in the moment and damn the consequences, but lately, she had noticed a streak of restraint and caution entering her world.

She turned off the town's main drag, parked the car, and got out. The town museum was a Victorian mansion turned into an Edwardian with the addition of a cupola and dormer windows. At the end of the 19th century, it had been the home of a lawyer and businessman who had made his money in mining and the railroad.

She trotted up the broad steps to the front door of the museum, admiring the image of a seagull in the stained glass over the front door, oblivious to a nondescript car pulling into the driveway.

Inside, a fossil of indeterminable carbon dating greeted her with a vapid smile. "We close in a few minutes, dear."

"I won't be long. It's important. Have you seen this woman before?" Jennifer passed the woman the picture of Caroline.

While the woman studied the photo, Jennifer scanned the interior of the house. The parquetry floor had area rugs with little wear. Immaculate wainscoting stretched from the front door to the kitchen at the back of the house. Black and white family portraits from the previous century hung above it, each family member staring back like ghosts.

"She was doing a story about hidden treasure," Jennifer explained.

The woman looked at her watch and tapped her foot. "Why would she come here?"

"You don't recognize her?"

The senior citizen smiled demurely and shook her head. Jennifer studied the woman's face, trying with all her might not to plaster her badge into the smug woman's face.

"Do you always work at the desk, Margaret?" Jennifer said, noticing her nameplate for the first time on the counter.

The woman grimaced. "I've been here every day for the last twenty years, rain or shine."

She waved her hand behind her head. "No one enters here without me knowing."

Jennifer asked if she could take a quick peek inside. The

woman batted her eyes as she weighed her options. The detective had to flash her badge to enter amid the woman's pleas to be swift.

The museum was more of a home with rooms preserved to capture the era's typical furnishings and lifestyle. The first-floor rooms featured Newel lamps, Tiffany lamps and boxes, Morris chairs, Chippendale blanket boxes, and hordes of other antiques.

Jennifer went up the servant stairs in the kitchen to the second floor. The bedrooms evoked an era of genteel country folk quoting from Byron and Keats in fireside chats. She ran her fingertips along the shellacked tops of numerous kinds of tables and the contours of bedposts and highboys made of walnut. Dressmaker mannequins in bowknot dresses to housemaid aprons stood in each bedroom.

Margaret called from downstairs. "I'm locking the front door now."

She found a picture on a dresser in the master bedroom. It was a very old picture of a young girl in a frilly dress with an accompanying newspaper clipping on the wall.

***The Stanstead Sentinel**, November 1938*

Eleanor Engleside, eldest daughter of the Engleside family, visiting Heidelberg, Germany, as part of a European trip to visit famous landmarks and religious houses across the continent. The trip was partially funded by the Ladies' Auxiliary for the betterment of young women. . . .

Margaret entered the room surreptitiously and startled the detective. "Have you found what you are looking for, officer?"

Jennifer recovered her wits and glared at the octogenarian. "I found this interesting article," Jennifer said.

"Yes, she was a lucky girl for her age. She looks rather unhappy in the photo, though," Margaret editorialized with a high tone in her voice.

Jennifer studied the plaque on the wall. "Can you tell me any more details?"

The old woman scrunched up her nose. "She was a bright girl, considered the religious life for a while until her father straightened her out. She ended up marrying a businessman who later cheated on her with his secretary or something like that. Tawdry affair all round."

Jennifer's eyes narrowed as she considered how the woman had lasted so long on the job with such an attitude.

The old woman tilted her head and crossed her arms. "I *must* ask you to leave now."

A sudden idea popped in the detective's head. "Did you have a visitor, a man, very stern, about forty dressed in designer clothing visit in the past few days?"

The woman hesitated, looking at her watch. A few moments passed. "If I answer, will you please leave?"

Jennifer agreed.

"Yes, some man with a tan. He told me he was a historian or something, but he looked too slick for that."

Jennifer described Brent's appearance in detail.

"That's the man."

"One final question, I promise, and then I will leave."

Margaret sighed and waved her hand in defeat.

"Do you know about the book, The Secret?"

The octogenarian's face brightened. "Oh, you mean, The Secret: A Treasure Hunt? I heard in the news about a probable location in Montreal at the Mount Stephen's Club. Why?" Margaret said.

"The gentleman you saw may be searching in the area for clues."

"Well, he's not a very good treasure hunter because the illustration in the book clearly identifies Montreal as the location. It's curious though only three have been found so far."

"You seem to know a lot. I'm impressed."

Margaret beamed. "Well, I just know what a friend told me. He was at the monastery last week and heard a talk about it," Margaret said.

"Really?" Jennifer said.

"Yes, apparently, Dom Chevalier invited them. I wonder about that man sometimes. He doesn't sound like a proper dom."

Jennifer opted not to pursue the line of inquiry any further and thanked the woman before leaving. As she went down the steps of the museum, a man exited the nondescript car while his partner remained behind the wheel. She caught sight of him heading her way and regretted not parking her car closer. She increased her pace.

He woke up, his mouth gagged and his hands and feet tied. He lay in the bed of a pickup truck as rocks ricocheted off the fender tubs, engine roaring and the vehicle pitching and heaving. He strained at the bonds to build up a layer of sweat, one of Houdini's tricks.

The truck lurched to a halt. The doors creaked open and slammed shut. Two sets of footsteps approached. One set of hands grabbed him by the wrists and the other set grasped his ankles, and he was carried a short distance before being thrown through the air. He landed with a thud on a hard, uneven surface. Dazed and still weak from the gas, he heard the sound of a seagull. A man grunted something unintelligible. They lashed something to his feet and placed him in a rowboat. He felt forward movement. The truck started and drove off. Silence descended over the lake.

For a moment, Bevyn felt all over again the despair that submerged him when his wife died—an awful wave of desperation that obscured hope. But a force from deep inside him surfaced just as the water reached his mouth. Resolve took over.

He loosened the bonds around his wrists and freed his hands just as his head went underwater. It revitalized him. He doubled his efforts and yanked his pocketknife from an ankle bracelet he kept hidden under his socks, slashing the rope around his ankles, once, twice, three times. His lungs were about to burst when, at about ten feet, he finally severed the cord and swam to the surface.

His head popped out of the water, and he ripped the gag from his mouth and gasped for air. After half a minute of spitting up water and coughing, he noticed the moon in the night sky. The lake remained quiet as a mausoleum. He felt elated and glad to be alive.

He reached the shore drenched and shivering, aware of the hypothermia risk. With his smart phone waterlogged, he assessed his predicament as dire, but always curious, he spotted truck tire grooves in the sand. He bent and examined them under the moonlight.

He followed the ruts to the main road, walking fast to keep up his body temperature. He also did something he hadn't done in a long time: he prayed. A number of cars passed until an old man in a rusted out minivan stopped and offered him a ride. The man was unshaven, smelled of manure, tended to be curt, and was an organic farmer. Oblivious to his passenger's ratty appearance, he rattled on the whole way back to the mansion about how agribusiness, the government's bed partner, crushed the little guy and how climate change was the earth's death knell. Bevyn arrived at the mansion fully intending to go totally organic and to cut his carbon footprint.

The guests didn't even notice Bevyn's dishevelled appearance. After a quick shower and change of clothes, compliments of the servant's quarters, he went for medical attention for the gash on his head dressed as a cook. A man sat at the medical desk, the clock behind him indicating 10:33 p.m. He yawned as Bevyn asked for a nurse.

"How can I help you?"

Irritated at the man, he switched to French and repeated his question. The man pursed his lips and exhaled, his breath ruffling his bangs.

"I *am* the nurse. How can I help?"

Bevyn apologized for his assumption. The nurse gave Bevyn a curt nod. "Happens all the time. Come in."

In the examination room, the nurse peered at Bevyn's head and then asked some standard head trauma questions. Bevyn steered the conversation to the weekend.

"I am only here on weekends. Mostly pretty boring stuff. You know, cuts and burns and stuff."

"Anything remarkable during our stay?"

"God, the cops want us to stay. Now they're saying that murder in the boathouse was real! I never thought this was a good idea—brings out the worst in people, if you ask me. You know, Freud and repression and all that."

The nurse prodded the contusion on the back of Bevyn's head. He winced. He followed up on his rhetorical question.

"Yesterday, someone came in with a black eye. He said he bumped into a cupboard, but I can tell a fist mark, you know?"

Bevyn chuckled casually. "I don't need to know," he said and made a halt sign with a hand.

Taking the bait, the nurse lowered his voice. "Good old-fashioned jealousy, if you ask me."

Conspiratorially, the nurse looked around and beckoned the professor closer. "The boss doesn't let, you know, *convention* get in the way when he likes a woman, if you know what I mean."

Bevyn spread out his hands and opened his mouth to speak, but the nurse prattled on.

"Same old, same old. But when you rub someone's rhubarb, that's pretty low. . . . Okay, no damage, but if you get sleepy or dizzy, report back to me. I'll be around, it appears."

The next day broke bright and fresh for the extended weekend. Sunday morning sunlight poured in through the library windows. Above each window, a famous detective's name had been engraved: Poirot, Queen, Holmes, Dalgliesh, Dupin, etc. Bevyn and Murphy huddled over a table between two stacks of books.

"Roy located the tire treads, just like you said. Japanese manufacturer. Roy's on it. How's the head?"

Bevyn shrugged his shoulders. "I might be sore for a while."

Silence fell between them as they looked at the illustrations in The Secret. Murphy studied Bevyn's face and rubbed his hands together.

"Maybe, Caroline was involved in this somehow," Bevyn said.

"Hmm, I'm sure lots of people from around the world are looking for the treasure." Murphy rubbed his jaw.

Bevyn straightened his back and stretched his arms upwards, letting out a groan of relief. "We have a case of mistaken identity perhaps."

Bevyn revealed his suspicions about the possible links in the case between the treasure hunters, Bob and Caroline, not to mention, the evasive superintendant, Clint. Murphy smiled. "Wait until the SQ finds out about all this mess."

"I'm sure it's just a matter of time before we sort it all out." Bevyn tapped on the tabletop.

Murphy poured over another picture in the book. "Our next move is obvious. We go public."

Bevyn stood up and began to pace. "I don't like it."

The older man sat back in the chair and pretended to

remove lint from the lapel on his jacket, giving the English literature professor a moment to digest his intentions. He toyed with the molar at the back of his mouth with a finger too.

Roy trotted into the library and broke the tension. "We find truck near Eustis mine. Stolen yesterday. Tires match." He watched their reaction.

The chief reached farther into his mouth with his other digits and winced. He removed his hand and faced his subordinate. The clock on the wall ticked off the seconds.

"SQ hold everybody. No one can leave," Roy said and clucked his tongue.

Bevyn sat down at the table again. "We know."

"I tried to stick to the plan, but these guys . . ." Murphy studied his fingers.

"Doesn't matter," Bevyn replied."

Roy made a sarcastic remark. Bevyn gave Murphy a flick of his head.

"It'll flush out any suspects," Bevyn said.

Murphy's face brightened. "I was thinking the same."

Roy let out an exclamation and dug inside his coat pocket. He produced a ticket stub and waved it like a winning 6/49 ticket. "We find this in the car!" Roy placed it on the table. It was a stub from the Stanstead museum. On the backside, someone had scribbled a phone number.

Bevyn nodded his head. "Interesting."

Murphy poked at the ticket. He motioned to his detective. "My glasses are in the office."

Roy nodded and picked up the stub. He slipped it in and out of his fingers, becoming more and more excited and riled up.

"It's obviously a phone number," Bevyn remarked.

Chief Murphy lifted his head. "Roy, care to enlighten us?"

Roy rubbed his nose and removed a smart phone from his pocket. "I call da number, Jones?"

"No one's going to answer."

"How you know dat, Professor Jones?"

"Because the phone is drying out in my room."

Murphy uttered a sound of incredulity, while Roy rubbed his hands together in triumph. Bevyn stared at one man and then the other, wondering more than ever about the plan and why and how

Caroline had gotten his number. He had just passed through the belly of the whale only to face friendly fire.

Chapter X

He had a late morning nap to shake off the effects of the previous night and dreamed of the monastery. In the dream, he climbed up through trapdoors and ladders, trying to escape unseen pursuers. They always remained a short distance behind, propelling Bevyn forward like a steer in a slaughterhouse. In the dream, Bevyn felt fear and anxiety and something worse: surrender. The pernicious feeling followed him to breakfast.

  Bevyn finished packing his bag for the tennis match with Bob. On his way to the courts, he checked his phone again. The time it had spent in the sand and under a hairdryer had worked. The phone operated as good as new. He remembered the episode on the river and shuddered.

  Bob arrived at the courts with Olivia. She carried his bag, racket handles protruding. He wore a set of designer shorts and a T-shirt with shoes to match. On his head, he wore protective goggles and a bright purple bandanna with a popular brand logo front and center.

  "I heard about your little adventure. Are you alright to

play?

Bevyn scanned Bob's face like a trained interrogation specialist. It was an Academy Award-winning performance by the manager. He managed to sound genuine with just a hint of sarcasm. Olivia reached up and touched Bevyn's head.

"Poor man. I can help you heal that faster."

"Maybe you should take a break from investigating and leave it to the big boys, there, Bevyn."

"Is it swollen?" Olivia murmured.

"Just a little, but a good night's sleep did me a heap of good. I'm fine to play."

"Are you sure? I wouldn't want you to permanently harm yourself."

Olivia touched Bevyn's head again. Bob reacted by asking for Olivia's help to locate his balls. She batted her saucer eyes and bent as she rummaged through his bag. She located the lost balls, and the opponents headed to the court. Olivia sat down on a bench and examined her nails.

After deciding on a one-set match, Bob served. A few bystanders grew into a small audience as the games went back and forth and Bob became frustrated with Bevyn's solid play. They reached set point with Bevyn up 40-30 at 5-4. With one swoop of his racket head, Bevyn placed the serve wide to Bob's forehand and came to the net. Bob whipped the return at Bevyn's head to the shock of the small crowd. Bevyn ducked, and the ball sailed long, out of the court. The onlookers applauded. Bob approached the net and shook hands with Bevyn and then he waved to the onlookers. He beckoned Olivia over, but she remained seated. Bob grabbed his bag and stomped off the court, headed back to the mansion.

Olivia stood as soon as he disappeared over the knoll. She joined Bevyn at the side of the court near a water fountain. Her freshly shampooed hair shone in the sunlight. "Bob's a sore loser."

Bevyn wiped his brow with a towel and took a swig of bottled water. "It was close."

"Will you join me for a little celebration?"

"Love to, Olivia, but duty calls."

She pouted as Bevyn took a step toward the mansion. Olivia touched his arm and murmured, "You need some TLC."

Bevyn patted Olivia's arm and thanked the people who had

come over to congratulate him on his play. He entered Bakerstreet by a back door.

Two officers stopped him near the entrance. Several small rooms had been converted into an interrogation area. Murphy overheard the commotion and shouted something in French. The officers let him pass. He found a very disgruntled Murphy in an alcove behind a small folding table.

Bevyn swept his hand through the air. "Looks like you got the executive suite."

Murphy cracked his knuckles. "Regular Ritz."

Bevyn placed his racket on the table. "We flush anyone out yet?"

They watched a young woman exit a room in a very short skirt, and Murphy pursed his lips. "*Nada*. How could you play tennis after last night?"

"Just a little bump on the head."

Chief Murphy spun a pencil around with his first finger and thumb. "Caroline stumbled onto something, I think. That guy, Brent, with the salon tan? He's definitely got some strange self-employment history and owes back taxes. Spent some time in the army, inherited a small antique business and went bust, but he moved on to buying and selling collectibles."

"What about Ivan, his buddy and the owner of the wallet I lifted?"

"Yeah, about that . . ." Murphy rotated his jaw in its socket.

"Won't happen again, sir. The friend?"

"Army buds."

Bevyn weighed the implications. His face lit up suddenly. "What about Bonnie and Clyde?"

"SQ got nothing out of them, yet."

The conversation stopped abruptly when Brent came down the corridor with a hockey player's gait, rocking from side to side. He held his head back, thrusting out a grizzled chin. He played with a smart phone in his left hand, sliding a pudgy thumb across the touch screen. Two officers stopped him. He swung his hands out, and the officers patted him down.

Bevyn stuck his face around the corner and spotted him. "How's your buddy's coffee stain?"

Brent ignored Bevyn's question and grinned, thrusting out

his chest and adjusting his shoulders. "Oh, I didn't recognize you there, Sherlock."

The chief rose from his chair and stood beside Bevyn, letting out an expletive on the way. "We were just talking about you."

The man adjusted the cuffs of his designer shirt and fiddled with the cuff links. "I'm flattered. But you're not my type, eh?"

The chief adjusted his belt. "And what type is that?"

The door opened and two SQ detectives came out, yelled a few words at the officers, and motioned Brent over. He made a rude sound with his mouth. "You think about it, Chief." He swaggered over to the room. The door closed after him.

Bevyn let out his breath. "Army time or not, he's a piece of work, that one."

"The SQ will give him a good going over, I assure you. By the way, they claim to know where the treasure in that book is and there's more."

Bevyn rubbed his hands together in excitement and started to pace on the industrial carpet. Murphy watched the professor go back and forth like he was a spectator at a tennis match.

"Brent and Ivan claim to know its whereabouts in Montreal."

Bevyn stopped, brought his fingers to his temples for a second, and faced the wall.

"Oh, and by the way, Olivia came looking for you earlier. She's got information," Murphy said.

Bevyn face broke into a smile. "I just beat her man at tennis. He tried to take my head off."

Murphy's manner lightened. "I don't wanna know. Anyway, she said she must talk to you pronto." Murphy pulled out his phone and looked at it. "The SQ has about twenty more to interrogate. We're no closer to the killer. On the upside, we can rule out Johnny Bell for sure." Murphy rattled off a few of the coroner's findings verbatim.

Bevyn peered out a window at the grounds. "What about the footprints?"

"We're going through all the guests. The boot pattern we lifted off the floor doesn't match Bell's. I've got a funny feeling it belongs to one of Bob's henchmen just like the one in the super's room. Any ideas about those numbers?"

Bevyn stroked his chin with his first finger and thumb. "Your guess is as good as mine. Make sure you check Bob's henchmen, Mack and that other gorilla. I'm going to see what the Lady of the Mansion has to offer."

"Be careful. The guests have to remain on the premises. They're not allowed to stray too far. So, you know what that means."

He fished inside his brain for past experiences, but came up empty. Murphy filled him in on the subject, even though the professor could have made an educated guess. It meant disgruntled guests, frustrated by the restrictions imposed on them, but it also meant they would be eager to help solve the case as soon as possible so they could go home.

Bevyn found Olivia in the kitchen, overseeing the meals for the extended weekend adventure. Bevyn caught her eye without even trying. She held up her first finger and then pointed to the foyer. Bevyn nodded. She arrived a minute later, brushing away a lock of hair from her forehead. She wore an apron with the phrase "Let's Get Cookin'" printed on it. She removed it and tossed it into a laundry basket. Her smile was radiant as she took Bevyn's hand and gently squeezed it.

"Sorry about that. Problems with tomorrow's menu."

"I didn't know you cooked."

She winked and wiped her hands on a dish towel. "I love to cook, Bevyn. You should know that by now."

"You wanted to see me?"

"Yes, I have something for you. I forgot to tell you. I was enthralled by the match! Ha! Anyway, let's go somewhere more private, shall we?"

"What's this about?"

"I've got important information I don't think you'd want everyone knowing about. I know just the place we can talk."

Bevyn followed Olivia down the corridor to a room behind the kitchen. She opened the door. "I think we'll be comfortable here. Would you like a drink?"

"Perrier."

"Fabulous." She retrieved a bottle of Perrier from a small

refrigerator. The bottle opened with a hiss. She added ice into two glasses embossed with the Bakerstreet logo and poured. She handed Bevyn a glass, and he took a sip. Olivia put a straw in hers, withdrew it, and licked it.

"I overheard some talk about that poor girl."

"When?"

"Friday night."

"Why didn't you say something sooner?"

"I remembered on my way back from that epic battle on the court."

Bevyn blinked, shifting his weight to his left foot, not sure where the duplicitous woman was headed with her information. "What did you hear?"

"I can't remember the exact words, but it was something like, 'She's going to find out everything.'"

"Who said it?"

"He was a handsome man, looked like an actor. I didn't recognize him because he was dressed like a soldier. He wore a hat low over his face."

Bevyn shifted his weight onto his other foot. "Could it have been Johnny Bell, the actor who died in the empty room?"

"I'm not sure. Maybe."

Olivia played with the rim of her glass, running her lips around the rim at an indescribable velocity. She put her glass down. "They were in a dark corner of the lounge. I overheard him talking to Mack."

The professor rubbed his cheek with the back of his hand as he pondered. "Let's say it was Johnny Bell. What would he be doing talking to Mack?"

Olivia's eyes opened wide, and she shook her head. Bevyn drank from his glass.

"What leads you to conclude they were talking about Caroline?"

"It's what he said to Mack at the end." Olivia took a few steps in Bevyn's direction, placed one hand on his shoulder, leaned in, and whispered in his ear like a schoolgirl, her breath warm and sweet and raising the professor's body temperature. "I heard him say, 'That reporter's asking too many questions. We got to do something.'"

Olivia lingered close and then withdrew, picking up her glass in celebration. Bevyn's heart skipped a beat. She swirled her tongue around the remaining contents of her glass and then swallowed the Perrier. She gave Bevyn a peck on the cheek on her way out.

Bevyn remained behind for a few more minutes, sorting through the latest information, speculating on Olivia's involvement—not as a suspect, but as a spreader of red herrings. Bevyn assessed Mack's potential involvement and the numbers he found in the office computer. Bell had gambling problems, and gambling and prostitution usually was the domain of the Hells Angels. Finally, there was Bob's mysterious list of numbers. There had to be a connection. But exactly what it was, he had no idea yet.

On his way back to the main floor, he assessed the converging plots and decided they all pointed to Caroline. Bevyn surmised that she had stumbled upon some of Bob's illegal activity and was going to go public, but he needed proof.

Chapter XI

Her captors strapped her wrists and ankles to a chair and left, leaving a bag over her head. She heard footsteps echoing down a long hallway, and a door boomed shut. Only the sound of the fluorescent lights' transformers broke the silence. The room smelled damp like the old cold room in the basement that her dad ferociously pulled apart one day when she was young.

She wrestled with the nylon straps. They cut into her wrists. No one responded to her calls for help. She gave up after a few minutes to save energy.

In hindsight, the events leading up to the abduction were so clear in her mind. The detective mentally kicked herself for her stupidity, but it had happened so fast. She had gone to her car after the museum, got in, and put the key in the ignition. Next thing she knew, a man had grabbed her by the hair and dragged her out of the car.

The door opened, a light went on, and someone removed the bag. A bare bulb hanging from the ceiling cast a feeble glow. She squinted at the two men in the room, one rotund like Humpty-

Dumpty, and the other, thin with a scar and biker gear and sporting a punk-ass grin.

"I hope you like the accommodations?" Humpty-Dumpty exclaimed in a raspy voice.

Jennifer grunted and spit on the ground. "Your customer service needs improvement."

"I'll lodge a complaint with the management."

As her eyes adjusted to the light, she saw graffiti on the walls. The high ceiling stretched upwards into darkness. The thin man moved behind her and started to play with her hair. She shook her head.

"Looks like we have a feisty one, eh, boss?"

"Blondes do always have more fun, eh, Sly?"

Jennifer squared her jaw. "Tell your boyfriend to keep his hands to himself."

The fat man made a slicing motion with his hand and approached Jennifer, while Sly cowered in a corner. "You changed your hair colour."

Jennifer smiled. "How're things, Poncho?"

"It's been lonely without you."

Sly guffawed and snatched a spider descending from the rafters. He placed the spider on Jennifer's head. She smiled at him unaffected by the intimidation. The thin man cracked his knuckles.

Jennifer shook her arms and winced. "Can you loosen these?"

Poncho nodded at the thin man. Sly stepped forward and then paused long enough to catch Jennifer's attention. He sliced the straps instead of loosening them and slipped a pocketknife into her hand, unobserved by Poncho.

Jennifer bit her lip and tilted her head back. "Does he always tell you what to do?"

Sly hesitated, eyed Jennifer's bonds and then nodded to Poncho. He stood up, the smile on his face gone.

"Do you need some water?" Poncho motioned in the direction of the door with his head, his eyes thin slits. Jennifer's new best friend moved at a snail's pace and exited. The door slammed shut with a monstrous boom.

Jennifer eyed Poncho. She felt cold all of a sudden. His eyes wandering over her body felt like slime oozing over her skin.

She suppressed a shudder. The fat man popped a pumpkin seed in his mouth and chewed with his mouth open.

"The doctor said they're good for my prostate. Why didn't you didn't tell me you were leaving? I could have sent you off in a pine box."

The door opened, and Sly returned with a bottle of water and handed it to the undercover cop. She took a swig, spilling water on herself. She wiped her mouth with the back of her hand.

"Do you know the definition of impossible?" Poncho answered his own question. "A blind man in a dark room looking for a black hat that's not even there."

Jennifer squirmed. "Your point?"

Poncho pointed at Jennifer and then at himself. "This is very complicated."

"I don't know what you are talking about."

It happened in a flash. The thin man raised his hand to slap her across the mouth, but the fat man stepped in and blocked it. The two struggled for a second until the fat man shoved his partner against the wall. Jennifer heard the air rush out of the thin man.

"I told you to let me take care of this, boss."

"You're gonna regret that, bub," Poncho said

Jennifer used the distraction to slice the straps binding her ankles. "No need to argue, boys."

The men stopped. She shook the hair out of her eyes and winked at Poncho. The fat man smiled at his partner.

"See, results."

"I'll make you a deal, Poncho."

Poncho let out a roar of laughter to which the thin man joined in at half volume. "Sure, sure, anything you want."

"You let me walk, and I keep my mouth shut," Jennifer exclaimed, gritting her teeth.

The fat man's smart phone rang. He answered it. He grunted some negatives and affirmatives and hung up. Frisbees replaced the pupils in his eyes. "We got company coming."

Sly didn't react. He kept his eyes on Jennifer.

Poncho pulled Jennifer's hair and spit in her face. "Looks like I missed a red flag."

"What's our next step, boss?"

"Kill her."

Poncho released his hold on the undercover detective's locks and bolted through the door. Seconds later, Sly removed his weapon. He waved it in front of her face like a lollypop. They heard Poncho's footfalls fade in the distance. She closed her eyes. The gun went off.

Just over the tracks on a hill, the Hells Angels' compound overlooked the St. Francis River that flowed into Sherbrooke. Tall fencing with razor wire on top surrounded the perimeter, and closed-circuit cameras covered every possible entry. Behind the main building, maples in colours Monet would have relished served as a contrast to the squalid and stark scene.

The SQ officers in charge of the operation watched the events unfold from a vantage point near the main entrance in a command vehicle. The SQ arrived with a ram, and the gate gave way. A special ops tactical team moved in with weapons at the ready. A car engine revved and barrelled out of a subterranean garage. The officers at the gate jumped out of the way as the car crashed into the ram. It reversed and squeezed between the gate and the vehicle. Some members of the special ops team let off a barrage of rounds from their automatic weapons, bullets bouncing off the car's armour. Two patrol cars gave chase as the car sped off down the road.

The compound surrounded, an SQ commander spoke into a bullhorn and demanded surrender. Someone inside retorted with a *clack-clack-clack!* of a large-bore weapon from an upper-story window. Special ops members responded with several rounds of ammo. Glass shattered as tear gas canisters sailed through the windows, launched from points around the building.

The SQ commander yelled a series of guttural directives into his walkie-talkie. A large bang echoed in the woods as the back door imploded. Seconds later, the sound of another exit tumbling reached the ears of the officers outside the command vehicle and then an odd silence descended over the compound. Without another gunshot, the special ops team emerged with the building's inhabitant, who hacked and coughed profusely. The faint sound of a spurt of gunfire broke the pall. The SQ commander listened intently to his walkie-talkie. It squawked, and he sighed with relief.

Jennifer emerged last, handcuffed and flushed with anger, led by the thin man. An officer relieved Sly of the prisoner, dragged her to a patrol car, and pressed her into the back seat. The car drove off. The commander approached Murphy and Bevyn, who sat in a police car across the road in an abandoned lot.

"Is she under arrest?" Bevyn blurted out.

Murphy ignored the question as the commander of the operation approached the driver's side of the patrol car. The chief rolled down his window. They shared a few words in French and then the commander left to supervise the shuttle of prisoners to headquarters.

The chief watched the smoke rising over the compound, and without looking at Bevyn, he remarked, "She'll be fine. She made the operation a success."

"I get it, but I don't understand. I thought she's one of yours."

"It's complicated."

"I don't need to know everything, but tell me where she's going."

Murphy tightened and relaxed his grip on the steering wheel. "It's confidential. I'll try to find out through my channels." He drummed his fingers on the wheel. "We have a situation back at the office that needs your expertise."

The chief shifted uncomfortably in his seat, tapping his fingers on the steering wheel before proceeding. He explained that Caroline's mother was at headquarters. The family had become suspicious about not being able to view the body. He removed his cap and tossed it on the dash. "She's dug in her heels and won't leave."

Bevyn swiped some dust on the dashboard with a digit. "She probably knows about Caroline."

The chief processed Bevyn's remark. "Look, I just need you to talk to her."

"Why haven't you told them the truth yet like I suggested?"

Murphy coughed and cleared his throat, gripping the steering wheel tighter at the same time. "I was hoping we'd have this thing cleared up."

Bevyn gazed at the sight of the earlier action. A melee of policeman and SQ officers swarmed the compound. A traffic cop directed rubberneckers to speed up. The words "carnage" and "war zone" came to the professor's mind although he had never fought in a war like the soldiers who had fought in the World Wars and more recently in Afghanistan.

Murphy started the vehicle, and they headed back to the cop shop. Murphy hummed a little tune, while Bevyn checked the saved texts again on his phone. Ladybug had been silent, and he wondered why.

Caroline's mother sat in a room off Murphy's office. The boys had brought her coffee and reading material. She glowered at Bevyn when he entered and sat down. He noticed the crow's feet around her eyes and her haggard and pale complexion. He swallowed hard.

"How's the coffee?"

She lifted her hand and rocked the mug, pointing at the sludge on the bottom. "Better than crankcase oil, I guess." She exclaimed sharply, "I'm here about my daughter."

Bevyn braced himself for the next few minutes. "Yes, ahem, Mrs. Samuels, Caroline . . ." He faltered, trying to think of a way to ease into the secrecy surrounding Caroline's body.

Mrs. Samuels frowned and placed the mug into her lap. Overhead, fluorescent tubes buzzed, and a slight breeze blew in through the aluminum windows.

"I . . ." Bevyn began, switching tack with the revelation.

Mrs. Samuels directed her eyes across the room. "Caroline contacted me. What I want to know is why someone tried to kill her."

Bevyn released his breath through his front teeth and leaned back in the chair. "So, you know?"

"She called me soon after that poor girl . . ." Mrs. Samuels choked on a sob.

The elderly woman dropped her gaze and fidgeted with the mug in her lap. She placed it on the desk. Murphy glided past the door and peered in for a second. Bevyn frowned, and the chief did his best impression of a casual passerby.

"What did she say?"

"Just that she had to go into hiding, someone was out to get her, and that someone had been killed in her place."

Bevyn's ears pricked up. "She told you that?"

The woman nodded. Bevyn considered Caroline's claim again that someone was out to get her. He needed to grill her about the treasure hunters and Bob as soon as he finished with the mother. She had obviously stumbled upon something.

"What you think?"

Mrs. Samuels shrugged her shoulders. An old railroad clock struck noon in the squad room.

"Why didn't you tell us about your family history?"

Mrs. Samuels back stiffened. "That's the past. I want to know about the present. Where's Murphy?"

Bevyn lowered his voice to a whisper. "I understand that Caroline's father was an important businessman."

"A sperm donor who got what he deserved."

Bevyn's cheek twitched. He leaned forward into the woman's space. "His wife investigated his death."

"They hoped to pin the accident on me by calling it a murder."

"And was it?"

"What are you implying? That I killed him? Why would I? I had plenty of chances, but never had the nerve. But why am I telling you? You know all the facts. So, you tell me, Mr. Jones."

"Seems Caroline inherited some money when he died."

The elderly woman removed a tissue from her blouse pocket and dabbed her nose. The wind picked up and blew the curtains out and upward in rapid motion, buffeted like a kite.

"The family fought it and won. It was guilt money anyway for his, um, predatory nature with women."

"He lied to you about being married?"

Mrs. Samuels recomposed herself in her seat. "No, I spoke out of turn." She exhaled. "Are you going to tell me who tried to kill my daughter?"

"The past may have something to do with it." Bevyn pressed the woman. "Now might be a good time to tell me the whole story."

"Shouldn't you be looking for that poor girl's killer?"

Seconds elapsed in complete silence. Bevyn heard the old woman's intestines protest against the lack of food or nerves. He assessed her, weighing the pros and cons of pressing her further.

He changed tack.

"What did Caroline think of her benefactor?"

Mrs. Samuel shifted in her seat. "She was angry, of course, but with me! She called me all kinds of mean things for getting involved with such a 'capitalist pig'. Those were her exact words."

Bevyn put his palms on the table and spread his fingers. "Let's leave that for now. Who would want Caroline dead?"

"How would I know?"

Bevyn handed the woman a document he had been holding in his hand.

"What's this?" Mrs. Samuels screwed up her face.

"You tell me?"

She opened the file cover and examined the papers in the folder. The elderly woman shook her head and closed the cover. "I don't know anything about it."

"Do you remember Jennifer, Caroline's friend from college?"

"Yes, she stayed with us a few times."

"What do you know about her?"

"Nice girl, pretty eyes and hair. They double-dated a lot."

"Did Caroline ever mention having been in COBA?"

"No, never heard of it. I'm sure she must have been undercover for a story she was doing."

Bevyn drew his hands back off the table and folded them across his chest. Bevyn realized Mrs. Samuels would offer nothing more, and he capitulated. He got up and went to the door hoping to find an officer, but the squad room was empty. All the officers had gone to lunch. He offered the woman a lift home. Mrs. Samuels declined, claiming she preferred taxis. Mystified by the quick end to the conversation, she exited the room like a doleful lamb.

Bevyn remained in the office for a few minutes, running Mrs. Samuels's disclosures through his mind. He was so engrossed in his musings that he failed to notice the chief's entrance.

Murphy's loud voice broke his train of thought. He congratulated Bevyn for vacating his office of the woman and demonstrated his gratitude by inviting Bevyn to a working lunch.

Chapter XII

Murphy sat in his old oak office chair and leaned back, clasping his hands over his stomach. He studied Professor Bevyn Jones across from him. He didn't regret his decision to allow the professor to join the investigation. In Murphy's mind, the only difference between an amateur and a professional was that a professional got paid.

They munched grilled chicken and teriyaki sandwiches from the trattoria next door. Bevyn ate while sliding his thumb across the face of his resurrected smart phone. Bevyn took a swig of the green tea he carried in a stainless-steel container. Murphy studied Bevyn's face for a sign of imminent vomiting.

The professor inquired about Caroline's location. Murphy removed a piece of red pepper from between his teeth before answering.

"She's in a safe place."

"It's time we talked to her about her biological father and what she knows about the treasure hunters and Bob."

"She refuses to talk and says we are just going to bring the house down on her."

Bevyn poked at his sandwich and extracted a browned piece of lettuce. "I've heard of COBA." Bevyn's expression lightened. "A friend of mine was a member in the late '70s. We thought he was nuts."

Murphy tapped on his chair with his fingernails. "I got some news on Detective Watson. She's officially dead in lieu of protective custody."

Murphy loosened the belt around his slight paunch. He pulled out a personal organizer. He tapped the functions before replying. "She's been working undercover for a year on the Hells Angels."

"Why is she at the retreat?"

Bevyn gave Murphy the once over while the chief toyed with the organizer. "Under cover. She's tough, that's all I can say." Murphy's voice trailed off.

Bevyn's phone rang. It was Jennifer.

"Sorry about all this."

"I always thought you were a woman of mystery."

She paused at the other end of the line. He heard the sound of a man's voice and the screech of a high-frequency wave.

"Talk later. I got some things to take care of first." The line went dead.

He stared at the phone like it was covered in mutant bacteria.

"I only found out about her involvement in the covert operation today. I mean, I recognized her at the mansion, but . . ."

Bevyn twirled his finger in the air, unimpressed. He paced the room. "No worries. I've got to pick up the scent again."

"Where you gonna start?"

"As always, 'in the library with the candlestick.'"

Murphy whistled and crumpled a piece of paper and tossed it in a basket. "I can save you some time."

Bevyn stood up straighter. Murphy rummaged through some folders on his desk and found the one he wanted. He handed it over. Bevyn lifted the cover of the file, and his eyes popped when he read the contents. "How on earth did you get this?"

"Does it matter?"

Bevyn closed the door and sat down. He read the text in

silence.

Murphy tapped a dated computer screen perched on a corner of his desk. "It came over the internet, by email."

"From who?"

Murphy scratched his head. "Ladybug."

"I'm beginning to think Caroline is Ladybug." Bevyn shared his suspicion with the chief.

The telephone rang and Murphy picked it up. He grunted a few derisive and indescribable sounds loudly and hung up. Their conversation continued where it left off.

"Why would she send texts?"

"I dunno, but I think we need to find out."

Murphy nodded and took the file back from Bevyn. He opened it and leaned back, lifting his head only for a second to watch Bevyn pass through the doors of the squad room. He made a quick call on his cell phone.

Shafts of late afternoon sunshine blended with orange-tinged vine leaves clinging to the mansion's brickwork to create a blaze of fall colour. He heard the sound of a gunshot in the woods across the lake, indicating that crossbow season had ended. Another deer with wasting disease had been gunned-down for meat or sport.

The front door of Bakerstreet opened and Mack, Bob's muscle man, came down the steps with a Rottweiler at his side.

"I see you made a friend."

Mack laughed and spoke to his dog. "He loves intellectuals." He relaxed his hold on the leash, and the animal barked.

Bevyn suppressed the urge to drop the gorilla with a deft blow. He disliked arrogance or bullying in any form, but the dog made it impossible to teach the muscle man a lesson in humility with aikido. He dashed up the steps to the front door and yanked it open. Mack pulled out his smart phone.

Bob intercepted the professor on the way to his room in the pool house.

"Jones, we cleaned up your quarters. It looks like a cyclone hit it. Whatever were they looking for?"

"I don't think it was dust bunnies."

The corners of Bob's mouth went south. Bevyn brushed

past the manger. Bob was prevented from chasing after the insolent amateur investigator by the sudden appearance of an inebriated rotund man who was complaining loudly about the confinement.

He reached the pool house. To his dismay, the mansion staff had piled all his personal items in a heap on the bed. Sheets, pillows, clothes, and everything else rose halfway to the ceiling. Unperturbed, Bevyn retreated and headed to the boathouse.

After jimmying the police padlock securing the door, he combed the interior, looking in every nook and cranny, even probing the water's depths, but nothing turned up until he saw it—a tiny piece of black material wedged between two floorboards. He used a pair of tweezers to retrieve it.

He withdrew after poking around some more. As he was snapping shut the padlock, he noticed another boathouse a few hundred feet further along the shoreline, partially hidden by a fir. Curious, he ambled over to it and quickened his pace when an idea struck him. The owner had secured the structure with a huge industrial-sized padlock. Undaunted, Bevyn went to work, and in a minute, he had the door open.

He snapped on an LED flashlight that cut through the gloom. Two kayaks filled one berth and a canoe the other. The placed smelled of old gas and canvas. The wood creaked underfoot as he moved about. He found nothing but empty beer bottles and fishing tackle. He called Jennifer from inside.

"I hear you're officially dead."

"Right, most interesting. I was just going to call you to meet."

"The trattoria on the second floor."

"Got it. I'll be dressed as Miss Marple."

Before Bevyn had the chance to respond, she hung up with a loud click. His head spun as he obsessed over Jennifer's exact involvement at Bakerstreet. Didn't detective Watson take particular interest in Shawna? Maybe, Bob was more her target. He would ask her when they met. Far more concerning, however, lingered the fact that the sound of Jennifer's voice had revived his spirits.

He found her in a dark corner of the eatery, hanging over her food like a flamingo. A few guests milled about, frustration showing on their faces about their delayed departures. Against the background chatter, Bevyn heard a Mozart ring tone. Jennifer's face was wrinkled, and her hair was done up in a bun and she wore a black Victorian dress with lace around the neckline. But underneath the disguise and makeup, her eyes looked marvellous, shiny and iridescent.

Bevyn slipped into the booth, mesmerized by Jennifer's costume. They scanned the room at the same time, like identical twins. The server welcomed the newcomer with a tilt of his head from the bar.

"What's that you're drinking?"

"Chai latte." She leaned back and relaxed into the cushions. "The SQ think you may have something to do with this." She leaned forward and whispered. "Roy's been talking to them."

Bevyn shrugged, and he rubbed his chin. Jennifer studied her companion for a moment and then took a sip from her mug.

The server came over to take Bevyn's order. He passed on Jennifer's beverage choice and selected an espresso instead. He hummed a little tune. "You're a sight to behold."

Jennifer wrinkled her nose. "How are you feeling? I heard what happened."

"I'm okay. Murphy filled me in about your undercover work for the Mounties. How are you doing?"

"I'm fine. I wanted to tell you, but—"

"Tell me about your afternoon at the museum," Bevyn interrupted.

Jennifer summarized her findings with little emotion, still embarrassed by the ease of her abduction.

Bevyn leaned over the table. "You should be in protective custody. These guys are the real deal."

Jennifer made a face and peered out the window. She brought her gaze back inside and stared at the dimple in Bevyn's chin. She lowered her voice. "I have a lead."

Bevyn leaned closer, the smell of her body lotion doing tricks to his head.

"Caroline talked to someone you might be interested in. It's in her diary."

Bevyn gazed at one of the guests dressed in a Charlie Chaplin outfit, complete with cane and hat. Mack passed the entranceway and took a quick look around and moved on.

"*Rewind.* How did you get her diary?"

"It's not important. Caroline mentions a woman she interviewed. She doesn't say what it was about, but she wrote down the woman's number. I called the number. It's the number of the caretaker at the museum, Margaret."

Bevyn brought his eyes back to Jennifer. Her holster harness crossed her body, cinching her breasts. She sipped the dregs of her latte.

Bevyn cleared his throat. "What on earth . . . What's she got to do with this?"

"I don't know, but she agreed to meet with me in North Hatley. She said she may have someone watching her."

The server arrived with his order. They discussed strategy and whether Bevyn should attend the meeting. After due consideration, the professor downed the espresso and slapped some coins on the bar on the way out, paying for both their orders. They reached the parking lot, and they both started for their cars. They solved the impasse by flipping a toonie.

As Bevyn drove to North Hatley, he brushed Jennifer's knee twice while shifting into sixth gear before she moved her leg. Bevyn didn't know whether to be happy about it or not. He was still mulling over the implications when he pulled the car into the Pilsen Pub located at the head of Lake Massawippi. He parked the BMW around back, and they went in.

A doorman greeted them, directing them to the pub on the lower level since the restaurant hadn't opened yet. Heavy Tudor style tables and chairs filled the room, which was complemented by a long aged wood bar and a low ceiling. A ship's wheel hung over the bar, and lights made with old harrow wheels hung from the ceiling.

The waitress seated them at a table along a bank of windows a few feet from and above the water's surface. The water was dark blue, leaves bobbing in and out of troughs.

"The last time I was here was for a first date with this guy called Zac, a graphic designer with a video gaming company. My friend fixed us up. She saw his profile on Facebook and sent me a link. It presented an out-going and creative guy with a calm exterior. It was the last time I judged a guy by his profile or got set up by a friend."

Bevyn smiled nonchalantly, unsure what the story had to do with anything. He wondered if she was communicating a covert message. She retrieved her smart phone and announced Caroline's interviewee's imminent arrival.

The waitress took their orders. Jennifer opted for a goat cheese and roasted red pepper on flat bread with a Kilkenny, and Bevyn ordered a cauliflower crust gourmet pizza with artichoke hearts and grilled chicken. His beverage of choice was a Guinness.

Jennifer's phone rang. She spoke a few words and hung up. The duo endured an interminable minute in silence until the elderly woman with grey hair, high cheekbones, and sallow skin arrived. She sat down in with flurry of emotion and handbags.

"The great Bevyn Jones! I knew your mother. She would be awful proud of you!"

Bevyn welcomed the opportunity to talk fondly about his deceased mother. After some shared memories between the two, Jennifer entered the conversation and the topic switched to the lakeside town a few minutes until they could no longer avoid the white elephant in the room.

"Why did you lie to me? You met with Caroline," Jennifer said.

"She swore me to secrecy and I had another reason you will hear about." She fussed with her handbag. "She came to me with a story. I confirmed it."

Bevyn examined the elderly lady's hands. They were the hands of a curator and book binder, but also a gardener by the appearance of dirt under her left pinky. Jennifer studied the woman's facial features. "What did Caroline want to know?"

Margaret removed a piece of paper from her blouse and crumpled it up before replying. "I don't know exactly."

"Just tell us what you told her," Jennifer replied.

She leaned back before launching into her monologue. "Have you heard of the Incan gold taken by the conquistadors?"

Bevyn and Jennifer indicated with confusion that they had.

"As you both know, then, it has never been found. Some say it lies on the bottom of the ocean or it has been melted down. Others say it's just waiting to be discovered."

Bevyn opened his mouth to ask for clarification, but the woman raised her hand before he had the chance. "The point is that people do crazy things over buried treasure. I am sure you know that, but Caroline wanted to know about a particular treasure."

Jennifer curled her lips while Bevyn watched a pleasure craft pass on the water to maintain his patience. The server came with their food. Margaret asked for water and started her story while the other two ate.

"There's a group of us looking for a treasure connected with a book called, The Secret . . ."

"Yes, we know all about it and frankly, I am tired of hearing about it. Let's cut this short. Why is it so compelling?" Bevyn inquired.

Margaret rotated a coaster on the table with her fingers. She clenched her teeth and made a hissing sound sucking in air.

"Because some of are worried that it's getting a bit too competitive."

"So, there's some kind of rivalry?" Jennifer said.

"I don't know what to say, but, as the saying goes, 'All's fair in love and war . . . and treasure hunting'"

Margaret lowered her tone as an elderly couple arrived and sat down a few tables over. The museum curator continued while Jennifer asked questions.

"There have been death threats. Anyone who finds the treasure is, how to say, going to face difficulties."

"From who?" Jennifer asked.

"I don't know for sure, but there's that Brent fellow and his sidekick . . ."

Jennifer interrupted and described Ivan. The woman shrugged, unable to confirm the man's identity. She took a swig of water from a glass the server had brought.

"What did Caroline seem most interested in?" Bevyn said.

"All of it. I told her that many have claimed to have found it or are searching for it."

Bevyn interjected. "They apparently found it."

The woman waved her hand in dismissal. "I'm not holding my breath."

Margaret got up from her chair abruptly. "I must go, before they find me. The death threats are real." With a nod of her head to Jennifer, she glanced to her left and right and left without saying another word. Stunned by the woman's swift exit, it took a few moments before the two detectives spoke.

"What do you think?" Jennifer said.

"It could be a reason for Caroline receiving some attention, but murder?"

Jennifer took a bite of her food. "Well, I admit I don't see how it could be related. And let's face it; she seems very paranoid about the rivalry over the treasure. Death threats? Come on . . ."

Bevyn nibbled at a morsel of chicken as he considered Jennifer's remarks. Silence ensued.

Look what I found!" Jennifer said all of a sudden and reached into her cargo pants and smiled. She pulled out a book.

Bevyn's eyes rolled upward. "More from Caroline's diary, I presume?"

Jennifer's forehead furrowed, and she sat up. "Excellent deduction. Now listen." She swept the hair out of her face and opened the diary. She read:

> *July 14: The group is brutally honest. That new guy is creepy. He stared at me for almost the whole hour.*

Bevyn made a clucking sound with his tongue. Jennifer continued:

> *July 21: Another night and I think I'll have enough for my story. Higher Power? Are they kidding? If a Higher Power can change people, why can't a Higher Power stop the crap to begin with? I don't know about this stuff. The people seem honest, though. When's the last time I truly believed anything? So hard. Afterward, a few [of us] went out to eat, but I can't change gears like that, hearing other people share their guts and then talk about the weather. One more to go.*

Bevyn motioned with his fingers, and Jennifer passed him the volume. "Some kind of twelve-step group?"

Jennifer nodded as Bevyn poured over the text. He read aloud another entry in the diary.

> *July 28: I'm starting to see what happened as wrong. So*

long ago. Could William be right? Still, I dunno. Anyway, maybe I'll go back. That creep wasn't there tonight. What a relief! The other women seem to agree. Stay away from him!

Bevyn handed the book back to Jennifer, a confused expression on his face. She read to herself while he scratched his head. Jennifer dragged her eyes away from the text and gave her dining companion a frown. "What do you think?"

Bevyn raised his shoulders.

"They ran a rape kit. Nothing, remember?"

Bevyn tapped his brow with his fingers, and suddenly, his entire countenance beamed. "We've been so focused on the forest, I forgot about the trees."

"What's up, Bevyn?"

"I'm not sure, just a faint glimmer of hope. It may be nothing, but there's something I should tell you. It's about Caroline."

Bevyn peered at the elderly man and woman seated at the table nearby. Jennifer waited impatiently for Bevyn's next words.

"Margaret's story's fascinating, but we need to find out who this creep is that Caroline mentions in her diary. And as for Caroline, well, she may not be who she says she is . . . was." Bevyn grimaced.

Jennifer shrugged. "Of course. Is anyone?"

"Right." Bevyn changed his mind about revealing the truth about Caroline. "Anything else in that diary?"

"I haven't finished it yet. It ends in August."

"Why August?"

"That's when William broke it off."

"I think it's time I drop in on dear, sweet William."

"He lives in a nice little brownstone in the North Ward with his mother and dog." She frowned. "What about Brent and Ivan and the perilous treasure hunting business?"

"I've no idea, yet. But Caroline sure gets into the most eclectic mix!"

The server passed by and asked them about their meals. The interruption reminded them that their food was getting cold. They dropped the discussion and focused on eating and returning to the mansion.

Jennifer reminisced about her friend and of their times together. Life took people on such strange paths. She remembered Caroline in university, a driven person, never without something in her life to keep her busy. Had there ever been a hint of anything amiss? Jennifer took pride in her ability to listen and to be empathic. Did Caroline try to reach out to her, or, like most of her classmates, had she been too busy to notice anything outside her world? It was a question she didn't want to dwell on too much, for fear of the answer.

Chapter XIII

Emma barked as the stranger set foot on the property. The Border Collie reminded Bevyn of his own deceased dog. He had never before owned a dog with such a combination of fierceness and loyalty. He recalled their walks across the university campus and how she had loved to chase down sticks outside and play ball inside.

Williams' pet barked even louder when he knocked on the door. After some shushing and pleas from the master, the door opened to a quasi-obedient but hyper dog. Caroline's ex was dressed in an Argyle sweater and khaki pants. He shook the visitor's without much cheer. Bevyn followed the tandem into a solarium at the back of the house.

They talked for a while about Williams' work as an engineer with the LEEDS movement to build more efficient homes, the Border Collie dog breed, and about the work/life balance until they finally sat down on a settee.

Bevyn shared some of the latest developments in the investigation. He finished off with a plea for the man's help with the case.

"Of course, anything I can do."

"This may be uncomfortable, but it's crucial that we explore something." He paused and leaned forward as if he were sharing top-secret information. "Did you know Caroline was doing a story on twelve-step groups?"

Williams raised his eyebrows. "Sure, she even joked she should join one."

"Why?"

Williams' head went back a little over the question, and Emma whined. Bevyn noted the perspiration on the man's brow but chalked it up to his large frame.

"Shh!" Williams ordered. The dog stopped. "Well, she had issues, eh?"

"Can you be more specific?"

Williams rose from his chair and fiddled with a nearby prayer plant. He brushed the leaves and tested the soil with a finger. "I'd rather not talk about it."

"She kept a diary."

Williams let a leaf flop back in place and faced Bevyn. Bags under his eyes told the story. "You know then." He cleared his throat.

"Know what?"

"She always talked about sex, sex jokes, sex games, sexual innuendo. She talked so much about it; I told her she should be a sex therapist. She thought I was a bit anal." Williams sighed with his shoulders hunched over. "I didn't want to mention it before, her being dead and all."

Bevyn examined the health of various orchids. The man obviously had a green thumb. "Was she molested as a girl?"

Williams sat down and shook his head. "Dunno."

"She ever mentioned any weird guys in the group?"

Williams' manner changed. He stood up again and examined the condition of an African violet. Emma joined him, and he stroked her head. "She mentioned this creep, some guy called Steve. I dunno if it's his real name or not."

"What did he look like?"

"She didn't say, and I never asked."

Bevyn watched Williams snap off dead leaves from the

plant with ferocity.

"We'll find the guy who did this," Bevyn remarked.

Williams nodded, and Emma barked twice. Bevyn bid farewell and exited from the solarium door. The outside air smelled of wood smoke and was crisp. He called Chief Murphy and filled him in. After signing off, he called Jennifer.

A smart-looking member of the hospitality crew was wiping off tables as they crossed the mansion's main dining room threshold. They sat down at a table far from the guests present for the meal. Bevyn guessed by their countenances that most were making the best of the weekend despite the climate created by the police.

Bevyn related to Jennifer the facts he extracted from Williams. She listened with keen interest about Caroline's past. "She never ever said a word to me, but she did kind of go on about sex sometimes, come to think of it. But who doesn't when they're in their twenties and early thirties?"

"And after that?" Bevyn's phone rang. He smiled and looked at the number. He excused himself and answered.

"Mr. Jones, John Williams. I remember something. That creepy guy in the twelve-step group, you know?"

"Yes?"

"He lived in an apartment complex in town, and another thing . . ." Williams paused to take a deep intake of breath. "He had a tattoo of a hinge on his arm where the forearm meets the upper arm."

"A hinge?"

"Yeah, like door hinges. Does that help?"

Bevyn thanked Williams and hung up. Jennifer adjusted her wig and touched up her makeup in a compact. He was about to share the details with Jennifer when his phone rang again. It was the chief. Bevyn widened his eyes to get Jennifer's attention. She clued in, and he put his finger to his lips.

"Hello, Chief, what's up?"

"A heads up. The SQ is looking for you. Lay low." He suggested a few courses of action and hung up. Bevyn stared at his smart phone.

"What's wrong?"

Bevyn struggled to reply. "It was Murphy telling me the SQ is looking into my involvement."

"The police already have you on file."

Bevyn gave Jennifer a mortified glance like he had seen a ghost. He grimaced in the knowledge that he had underestimated the detective.

She put the compact away. "It's the times we live in. What used to be called a 'free thinker' is now considered a threat today. I never had you for a terrorist, though."

"I feel much better knowing you think so. How did you find out?"

"The SQ recommended I put some distance between us." She bit into some Brome Lake Duck with zeal and washed the mouthful down with coffee like a truck driver.

"The retreat invitation makes sense now."

"How do you figure?"

"They wanted me to create some controversy."

"Aw, come on. Don't get all bent out of shape. They just don't understand people who want to make a difference in this screwed up world."

"Here I thought I was invited for my amateur sleuthing abilities." Bevyn took a sip of tea as Jennifer massaged her cup of coffee with her thumb.

The dining area continued to draw people into the mid-afternoon. A couple dressed like aviators sat at a nearby table. They gabbed in rapid Arabic while a couple farther away ate off each other's plates.

"Anyway, the super was part of the twelve-step group."

Jennifer put down her mug. "Clint?"

"Williams remembered Caroline mentioning the hinge tattoo. We need to pay Clint a visit."

"Don't the cops have him under surveillance?"

"You tell me."

Jennifer gave Bevyn a face. "Drop the sarcasm. I have no idea, just like you."

Out of the corner of Jennifer's eyes, she spotted one of Poncho's men enter. He was dressed like a butler, but Jennifer never forgot a face. She slouched down in the bench seat. "We got company."

They slid out of the bench and moved to the back door. Once outside, they crossed the grounds in the opposite direction of the boathouse. After about a five minute walk on a path that paralleled the shoreline, they reached a small pier with a boat bobbing in the waves. Bevyn dropped into the driver's seat.

Bevyn responded to the question on Jennifer's face. "Call it an action plan. Just untie us, and let's get outta here."

Jennifer deferred to the urgency of the situation rather than legalities as Bevyn reached under the dashboard and hot-wired the boat. After a few agonizing sputters, the engine cranked over and then the inboard motor coughed, sputtered, and died. He paused and tried again. The engine caught, spewing foul blue smoke.

Jennifer yelled over the roar. "Where are we going? It'll be dark in an hour or so."

Bevyn couldn't hear her over the roar of the V8. He threw the throttle lever forward, and the boat shot across the waves. Jennifer shrugged and dropped her lithe frame into the boat and held tight. As the boat's prow rose in the water, Jennifer shook her head in amazement over how nothing could stop Bevyn once he got an idea into his head.

The sound of a familiar voice instructed the detective to get into the SUV as a bodyguard held the door open. The man sat down, an expletive on his breath as the door slammed shut. The detective was staring straight ahead while a very fat man was sipping from a glass of wine beside him. The interior smelled of leather and Old Spice.

"What do I owe the pleasure, detective?"

"Jones is on lake."

"Why should I care?" Poncho said.

"She with him, like I said. Alive."

Poncho offered Roy a glass of Merlot. Roy screwed up his face and glanced nervously outside at the gorilla. Poncho laughed over the detective's sudden concern with professional ethics and swished the red liquid around his mouth, savouring every red drop. He leaned back in the seat, drumming the armrest with his fingers. "Detective Roy, did you know wine's considered the nectar of the gods?"

Roy crossed his arms and muttered a series of expletives.

Poncho let out a huge laugh and removed a handkerchief from his pocket to wipe his brow. The detective looked the man over out of the corner of his eye. He remembered their first meeting at a bar on Wellington. He grew up with a romantic fascination for biker gangs like a lot of people, but the romance had been replaced by reality. They were just common criminals.

"Now, Roy . . . Can I call you Roy?"

Roy shrugged. The car was parked outside the pub, as conspicuous as a whore in church.

"I need your assistance to retrieve something."

Roy couldn't squash the heat rising to his face. He stared at Poncho. "You leave my family alone. We got a deal."

"Oh, come now. I'm a family man just like you. Just do what I say and there's no problem, *comprends-tu?*"

"I gave you what you want. Now, leave us alone."

Roy's raised voice brought the bodyguard to the open window. "Everything okay in there, boss?"

"Roy got something caught in his throat. Detective, we need each other, don't we?"

Roy removed his eyes from Poncho and pulled the door handle. "You got what you want. I don't know nutting." He pushed the door open and bolted from the vehicle. The gorilla moved to pursue, but Poncho yelled to desist. "We know where she is. Let's go."

The henchman slammed the car door. Roy jumped, taking it for a gunshot. He refused to run and calculated how many seconds it would take for a bullet to drop him. He sighed with relief once he was out of range.

Poncho spat out the car window. "She's worse than that babe who ended up with the Minister of Foreign Affairs. Find out where our men are."

Poncho's phone rang. He ignored it and focused on something so incredible and miraculous across the street under a large neon sign that his eyes grew in wonder: an invitation to sample Coaticook ice cream at a roadside parlour.

Bevyn steered the craft through the waves and across the lake. The dying light left streaks of gold on the water, and a few billowing sails dotted the horizon. The windscreen's dimensions allowed

Bevyn to feel the wind in his hair like he was on a motorcycle.

Bevyn reduced the throttle to a crawl. "We'll wait here for a bit. No one's following us."

Jennifer removed the wig, smoothed back her hair, and tied it into a bun at the back of her head. Bevyn watched the operation with fascination, entranced by the simple things she did that captured his attention.

Jennifer reached over the gunwale and dipped her hand in the water, reviving some sensuality she had lost because of recent events. She adjusted the holster under her camisole.

Bevyn faced the stiff breeze and vowed that after the case was solved, he would spend more time near the ocean and on the beach. In fact, he had a standing invitation to visit a friend in Costa Rica to lollygag along a white sand beach. Maybe he'd invite Jennifer. He could watch her do that hair thingy until the end of time.

Chapter XIV

Sunlight reflected off the new copper sheathing on the mansion's cupola as the boat drifted down the lake. Behind the building and above it, white birch trees pointed to the heavens, standing tall like gatekeepers. Typical Eastern Township's grey clouds hung low near the horizon.

The case had reached a point where the loose ends had decreased. Bevyn wondered more and more about the connection between the past and present. Jennifer noticed Bevyn thinking and asked for a plan.

Bevyn looked up and grinned. "We have orders." He shared part of the plan.

Jennifer shook her head emphatically and let out a slight moan. "Staying here much longer is not a good idea."

Bevyn tweaked his shoulders and lifted his smart phone, showing Jennifer the screen. "Poncho's been spotted."

Jennifer grasped the edge of the boat as a large wave rocked the craft. "So, this is about *me*."

Bevyn studied Jennifer's face. "The police set a trap for

him."

She went over and sat beside Bevyn. He brushed the hair out of his eyes. "We weren't going to sit around waiting for his men to come after you."

"That makes us the bait?!"

"They wanted to give Poncho the personal treatment. They informed me because they believe we . . . ah . . . are involved."

Bevyn reached over and touched her hand. "Sorry to keep it from you. We didn't have much time, but here's how the whole thing is supposed to go down."

When he finished, Jennifer arose and went to the back of the boat. "I don't like it."

Bevyn goosed the motor. He raised his voice above the rising RPMs. "No time to discuss. Sorry, not sorry. They left the dock two minutes ago."

Detective Watson took a position beside Bevy at the dash. He opened the throttle all the way. The boat gained speed and shot across the lake.

In a few minutes, they reached the designated spot near the lake's ending point in Vermont. Bevyn slowed and cut the motor. A Zodiac bobbed on the water nearby. A man stood casting a line, while his mate sat reading the paper. The standing fisherman tipped his cap. A few moments later, they heard the sound of a boat with a powerful motor headed their way. The men in the Zodiac adjusted their vests, checked their weapons, and gave a thumb up.

The boat approached with two men dressed in black, hunched down. One of Poncho's men, a stocky helmsman, cut the motor to an idle and drew the craft within a few feet of Bevyn and Jennifer's boat. The two had disappeared. Something landed in the bottom of their boat with a thud. The pilot gunned the engine, and the boat took off. The fishermen sprang into action. Their boat roared to life and raced after the speed boat. A police helicopter with men hanging from the doors with automatic weapons came out of nowhere. It descended and chased after the escaping gang members.

Meanwhile, to the horror of the handful of tourists and locals standing on the dock watching the drama, Bevyn and Jennifer's boat exploded into a ball of fire with bits of fibreglass and wood landing on the water with a hiss.

The chief's office looked like a records library with papers, file folders, and banker's boxes sitting on every available flat surface, even Murphy's chair. Roy showed up and was amused to see his boss on the floor flipping through a folder.

"Chief, they get 'em, but what are you doing?"

Murphy snorted like a bull. "Can't find that damn file on the death in the boathouse in 1970."

Roy muttered. "New Guy have it."

"Did he take it from my desk?"

"*Non*, you give him, boss."

Murphy stopped rummaging around, tossed the folder in his hands on a chair, and eased himself to a standing position. "Stop calling me that!" He hitched up his camouflage pants and adjusted his suspenders. "Send him in here."

"He out on assignment, boss . . . um, Chief."

The older man's eyes narrowed. "Where?"

"You send him to monastery to talk to . . ." He pulled out a notepad. "To find information about bad monk." Roy straightened up and raised his voice. "But I have bad news."

"I know. The SQ officially took the case off our hands today. The reason I came out of retirement and back here and it's been outsourced!" He pulled on his earlobe, brushed through the doorway, and headed to the bathroom. A few heads in the room swivelled as he went.

Roy called after the chief. "Poncho get away!" Roy waved his hands in the air.

Murphy dropped his head. "When, how?"

"At the border. They get one, but—"

"It was supposed to be a slam dunk."

"Jones and Detective Watson blow up. Boom!" Roy brought his hands together. The sound reverberated around the squad room. He rocked on his feet for a second, shame-faced and unsure of himself.

The chief let out a long sigh. "I thought it was a bad idea."

"*Tabernac*! They in wrong place, wrong time, *c'est tout*!" He opened his hands wide in front of his body.

Chief Murphy lifted his head, stared at the ceiling, and, to no one in particular, shouted, "I'll be in my office for *a while*!" He shuffled off to the bathroom.

Roy walked over to the New Guy near the top of the stairs. "*Le capitaine* want his file."

"Which one?" The New Guy's eyes roved over his desk.

"The boathouse one he give you."

"I gave it back to the chief."

"*Certain?*" Roy spat out an expletive that morphed into an f-bomb soliloquy.

The New Guy ransacked his desk, looking for the file. Roy backed away and gave the policemen in the room the evil eye. "See anyting funny here, people?"

The whole room went silent. Roy made an imploring face. "Nutting?"

A thin, rakish officer stood up from his desk. "Only person around here lately was that plant guy. I told him he had the wrong office since everything dies around here."

"He here long?"

"I dunno. I just noticed him near your desk with one of those carts filled with plants."

"Description?"

"Hard to tell. He was in baggy black cargoes and a sweatshirt, and he wore a black tuque. Short, maybe yay high." He gestured with his hand. "He talked kinda strange."

"Strange? Explain."

"Well, sir, like a girl." The skinny officer gestured with his hands the shape of an hourglass.

"Was he a girl?"

"I dunno, sir. I'm not sure."

The chuckles of the two other officers in the room were silenced by a wolf whistle. "Well, we get him on camera."

The detective cleared his voice. "Isn't one Detective Roy."

Roy swivelled his jawbone in its socket and put his finger to his nose. "*Pourquoi?*"

"Union, sir."

Roy threw his hands in the air, picked up a glass from a nearby desk, and brought his arm back to throw it across the room but stopped when everyone took cover. "*Tabernac!*"

Murphy came bounding out of the men's room over Roy's barrage of profanity, shirt flapping in the breeze and suspenders trailing behind. "What in tar-nation is going on!"

Roy stifled the urge to laugh and placed the glass on the desk instead. The words exploded out of his mouth: "*Maudit ostie affaire stupide.*" He sat down. Murphy reached behind his back and looped his suspenders over his shoulders. He fiddled with his shirt sleeves.

"I want details, people! Roy!"

An older officer with a receding hairline stood up. "Sir, what about Poncho?"

The police chief stretched his neck. "Stay in the loop with the RCMP." He stamped past Roy's desk and went to his office and closed the door. A few seconds later, the sounds of country music filtered through the walls.

The high-performance SUV approached the border station in the dark. The guard on duty waved it through. The two uniformed U.S. Border Patrol agents in the front seat bantered over a wild poker game the previous night. Bevyn and Jennifer sat in the back seat, wearing borrowed clothes.

Bevyn reached into his coat pocket and played with his smart phone. "That's two times for you and two for this baby." He brought the phone to his ear and said to the officers, "Any news on Poncho?"

One of the officers, clean-cut with a chiselled jaw line, replied, "We got the pricks on the water. As for the fatty, don't worry, we're closing in."

The vehicle stopped on the Canadian side of the border where they were transferred to an RCMP vehicle. The officers welcomed them aboard and chauffeured them back to the mansion, headlights cutting a swath in the pitch black. Conversation remained at a superficial level as the officers were not privy to the reason for the escort.

The SUV came to a stop at the back entrance of the mansion, as per Bevyn's request. Every window blazed with light like something out of a greeting card.

"The house looks rather eerie," Jennifer exclaimed after they thanked and bid their escorts goodbye.

Bevyn and Jennifer traversed the lush, green lawn by moonlight. Workers had wrapped up the fountain at the north end to protect it from winter. A man was walking his dog.

"You didn't tell me about your interview with Williams."

"He's hard to read. I think he's grieving, though."

"Her death or something else?"

Jennifer squeezed Bevyn's arm a little. He didn't flinch, and they continued along a path that wrapped around the house and led to the river.

"I called the twelve-step group's point person. She knows Clint but couldn't tell me anything about him. Anonymity is the name of the game in the group. He rarely joins the group for any social activity."

"Either he's shy or has ulterior motives."

"I learned more stuff, if he's our guy. Want to hear it?"

Bevyn urged her to spill.

"First of all, he hasn't been to the group in weeks."

Bevyn's phone vibrated with a text message. "Incredible! The thing works." He summarized the message. "They think someone entered the office and read the file on Peters."

"Is he the businessman who died in the boathouse?"

Bevyn nodded and slipped his smart phone back in his pocket.

"Everything's falling into place. Caroline is . . ."

"Caroline is what? You mind sharing there, Sherlock?"

"Almost ready, just a few more things to sort out. First, a visit to Mr. Hinges."

They paused at the edge of the river to watch two mallards with three chicks paddle in the water. A couple dressed like Goth wannabes danced near the water's edge. Jennifer eased a camera out of her purse and snapped a picture. It would make a great addition to her collection.

Early the next morning, after talking to the superintendent of the two apartment complexes, Bevyn and Jennifer located Clint in the dingier of the two—an early seventies three-floor box. They climbed the stairs to the second floor and knocked. They heard footsteps and his nasal voice. "What do you want?"

"Police," Jennifer announced through the tattered door.

They heard the clink of metal against metal, and the occupant opened the door a crack. The Bakerstreet super had shaved his hair off.

"We need to talk," Bevyn said.

"Don't you people ever quit?"

Jennifer stuck her badge in the crack between the door and the jamb. "We have a few questions."

The super grimaced and flung the door open, and sidled off deeper into the apartment, leaving the two detectives standing in the doorway. Bevyn and Jennifer crossed the threshold and sauntered down a dark and dingy short hallway. Black and white pictures of women in public hung on the walls. Clint lay on a bench in the living room in front of a sliding balcony door, ready to do some bench presses.

"I don't have to talk to you. My cousin's a lawyer."

"Then we understand each other," Bevyn remarked with a grin.

Clint flexed his arms. The hinges ballooned. "I told the coppers everything, eh?"

"Sure. We are just following up. Bevyn says your place at the mansion got pretty trashed.

He sat up and ogled Jennifer. "At least the cops are hiring real talent these days."

Bevyn pulled out a picture from his wallet and stuck it in Clint's face. "Do you recognize her?"

Clint's eyes blazed as he sized up Bevyn. "Sure, that's Nicole . . . or was her name Betty?"

"You haven't been going lately," Jennifer inferred.

"What's this about, eh?"

Bevyn remained near the super, just in case he tried anything. "She's no longer in the program."

Clint reclined on the bench again, lifted the barbell, and pumped off a few reps, exhaling and inhaling, the veins on his biceps pulsing. He let the bar down with a crash.

"Yeah, what of it? She came a few times and left."

"Apparently, you took a real interest in her at the group," Jennifer said.

"What of it? I like attractive women."

Clint saw the butt of Jennifer's handgun jutting out of its holster. He glided into the kitchen, where he opened the refrigerator door and retrieved a blender carafe. He popped open the top and took a swig. He gave his visitors a glance like a cornered fox, looking for avenues of escape.

"You often take pictures of women in public?" Bevyn said.

"I have a good eye."

"Visited family recently?"

Clint almost spat out the power drink. He wiped his lips with the back of his hand. He heaved his chest. "Unless you have a warrant or something, I have a set to finish."

"Where were you at 10:00 a.m. on Friday?" Jennifer said.

"Don't remember."

"The cops pulled you over for speeding."

"They were lucky to catch me."

"What were you doing there?"

"Funny thing, I'm blanking out on that one, detective," Clint said, slurring his words provocatively.

Bevyn studied the black and white prints on the wall. He traced the outline of a woman in one of the pictures with his finger. The super watched, the grip on the carafe in his hands tightening.

"I see you have a few pictures of Nicole or should I say Beth here. Was she your favourite?"

Clint took another drink, set the carafe on the counter, and swirled the green power drink around his mouth.

"Did Beth know about them?" Bevyn said, touching her picture.

Clint swallowed and strutted over and stood between Bevyn and the picture. He poked Bevyn in the chest. The professor reacted instinctively with an aikido move, grasping the super's wrist and bending it back, bringing the man to his knees.

"Tell us about Beth Bentley," Jennifer demanded.

Clint hissed through gritted teeth. "I don't know any Betty Bentley. Now let me go!"

Bevyn released his grip, and Clint sprang to his feet.

"I will be bringing charges against you bucko," Clint rubbed his wrists and considered slamming Bevyn against the wall to remove the annoying look on his face.

"You don't seem broken up about her death."

"I don't know what you're talking about," Clint said, his teeth clenched.

Jennifer pushed Bevyn toward the door. Mission

accomplished, they vacated the premises, Clint's f-bombs trailing behind them. Moments later, the door slammed shut, the sound echoing down the corridor.

When they reached the ground floor, Bevyn spoke first. "So, was it Murphy who told you about Beth or Roy?"

"It should have been you, Bevyn Jones."

Bevyn apologized and explained the reason behind all the subterfuge. Jennifer accepted it with some convincing.

"We were going to tell you, but—

Jennifer held up a hand impatiently and changed the subject. "I didn't like the way he was looking at me."

Bevyn slowed his pace and nodded his head. "Clint seemed like your typical punk at the mansion. But now, I'm not so sure. He suddenly sounds sketchy, like a Dr. Jekyll and Mr. Hyde."

"Something's amiss. He could have killed Beth, but why is the question and another thing, where's Caroline? Do you know?"

Bevyn explained Caroline's whereabouts as best as possible, that only Murphy knew her exact location since she feared for her life.

"I don't like being kept in the dark, Bevyn, but I can understand why things had to be done the way they were." She reflected. "Is her life really in danger?"

"The police are keeping her under surveillance just in case."

They climbed into Jennifer's car and headed back to the mansion in silence. As the car travelled down the road, Bevyn was wondering more and more about the twelve-step group and its participants, and whether Caroline could have entered police headquarters in disguise. At the same time, Jennifer was ruminating about Caroline's predicament and the young woman killed in the boathouse.

Murphy stood at the office door as the New Guy cleared out the paraphernalia. Roy stood beside him, alternately eyeing the occupants of the squad room and the New Guy. Roy lingered a few seconds longer and was about to leave when Murphy ushered him into the office.

The chief told the New Guy to scram, and he exited. Murphy indicated for Roy to sit, and he closed the door. "Good work. What happened at the monk-astery?"

"*Pas grand chose.* I talked to Dom Chevalier, and he not have many good things to say about Jones."

Murphy brought his hand down on his desk, palm flat. He picked up a pen. Roy made a face.

"Anything else?"

"Nutting. He think us crazy."

Murphy spun a pen around using only his first finger and thumb. Roy leaned back and cupped his hands around a knee. The chief scribbled notes on a pad of paper. Roy remained mum and glanced at Murphy, who sighed.

"I need your help, Detective Roy."

Roy studied his superior's rumpled clothes and balding pate and suddenly he felt sorry for the old guy. He liked Murphy, even the way he spoke French, and hated the others in the squad room for disliking him simply because he had an English name. Murphy stopped scribbling. Roy decided to not tell him about the missing file turning up in the can for some reason.

Murphy picked up the phone and dialled. "Mrs. Samuels, do you have a moment?" A wry smile came to his lips for a second. He winced. "Your daughter is safe. I want to talk to you about the inheritance. Can you tell me who was next in line?"

He bobbed his head and crossed his eyes to Roy's amusement. Mrs. Samuels's voice rose on the other end of the line. He used the pen to scratch the back of his head. He moved the pencil to his ear and dug for earwax. Roy diverted his gaze to his cell phone, unable to watch the excavation.

"I see, I see. Oops, got another call. Got to let you go, bye. . . . Jones! Risen again, good man! Yes, Roy told me . . . 'Reports of your death greatly exaggerated.' Yeah, from Mark Twain. Okay, the inheritance angle is . . . What's his name? Okay, good. Bye."

The mining operation over, the detective gave the chief an imploring face. Murphy rose from his desk and placed a hand on Roy's shoulder. "Jones and our man . . . ah, woman made it through."

Roy sputtered an expletive under his breath. "Jones not dead? But how dis possible?"

"You sound disappointed." The chief chuckled over Roy's obvious confusion. He showed no mercy by saying, "They walked on water."

Roy rose from his chair, peeved at Murphy's teasing. He changed the subject. "Remember about plant person? I got news. Desk sergeant say he see person get out of blue van."

Murphy went back behind his desk and sat down. "That narrows it down."

"We check now."

Murphy pursed his lips, and Roy hesitated at the door. "Ah, Chief. We not on case, no?"

Murphy leaned forward and blew a speck of dust off his desk. He smiled at Roy and adjusted his suspenders. "Technically."

Chapter XV

As the sun rose above the trees, the air lost its typical fall coolness, prompting some guests to go outdoors to enjoy the warmth. Inside, Bevyn and Jennifer casually circulated amongst the guests, noting anything out of the ordinary, which was even more challenging with everyone in costume. Bob bounced about like a kid waiting for his birthday cake to be served, insisting even after the second death and the interrogations that the show must go on.

Bevyn spotted the local colour: Mr. Holt and his spasmodic personality and politics—a mishmash of socialism and capitalism. He waved him over and introduced him to Jennifer. "Lawrence, how was the fishing today?"

The gentleman didn't recognize Bevyn at first for the second time, but the quizzical expression on his face changed to delight over Jennifer. "Miss Watson, the pleasure is all mine. Jones, is it?"

Bevyn feigned a bow, and the old man blurted out an apology. "Just didn't recognize you, I'm afraid. Vision and memory aren't what they used to be."

Bevyn placed a hand on the man's arm. "I'm sure your vision's better than most." The old man's face took on a puzzled appearance until he understood Bevyn's reference to wisdom that comes with age. He tapped his head. "Yes, quite, quite. Oh, sorry about the other day. I was put out a bit. You know, arthritis."

Bevyn witnessed Jennifer's face soften for the first time. The old man reached into his pocket and pulled out a medication pill and popped it into his mouth like a vitamin.

"Where's your wife?" Jennifer said.

The old gentlemen beamed. "Oh, she'll be down soon." The old man felt his leg. "Do you mind if we sit down?"

Bevyn and Jennifer nodded emphatically, and they went to the parlour. Bevyn requested water from a server who was passing by, and they sat in a bay window area facing the fountain outside.

"Where were we?" The man hooded his eyes. "The mansion. Well, in the late '40s, it was owned by one of the Engleside descendants, and he rented out the grounds to people for marriages and the like."

"Did you know him personally?"

"I talked to him on the phone, but we never met. We worked through his secretary once about renting the house for our eldest daughter's wedding."

"Did you know he had a daughter?"

"Just one? No, but I'm not surprised. I remember the son. Quite the athlete."

Bevyn removed a picture of Caroline from his pocket. "Did you see this woman Friday night?"

Holt took the picture and brought it close to his eyes. "Sorry, I can't say. She's pretty."

A flash of sunlight reflecting off a passing car lit up the room. Holt's face brightened all of a sudden. "But I remember a woman in a dress, a green dress, very attractive."

Bevyn and Jennifer exchanged glances. Bevyn leaned forward. "Did you say a *green* dress?"

The old man made an affirmative humming sound. "She danced like a klutz, bumped into my wife and me on the dance floor."

Jennifer tapped the man on his knee. "What makes you think it might have been her?"

"Well, she smiled, and her smile was as radiant as the one on the woman in this picture." He flapped the picture in his hands and then gave it back to Bevyn.

"Do you remember what time you saw her?"

He let out a loud belch and caught his breath. "Excuse me! Must be the tacos. Around 10 p.m. It was late, I remember. Late for us, that is. We usually go to sleep early, but once in a while, it doesn't kill us if we stay up late."

"One last question. Did the woman in the green dress act strangely in any way?" Bevyn asked.

"What do you mean?"

"Was she nervous or apprehensive?"

"She looked like she was having the time of her life." He rubbed his leg and arose. "I best go see what the missus is up to. Nice bumping into you, Sherlock. You, too, Watson." He chuckled at his own joke. His joints cracked as he stutter-stepped out of the room. Bevyn and Jennifer sat for a while in silence, digesting the new information.

Jennifer touched Bevyn's knee. "What's with the green dress? Caroline had a black one on."

"I wanted to make sure. Did you know that Caroline was in a cult for awhile?"

Jennifer searched her memory banks. "She did disappear off the face of the earth for a while. But a cult! No, she doesn't seem the type."

Bevyn let out a loud laugh, which got the attention of a few people in the vicinity. "There's a type?"

"Sure, you know, all serene and religious, like monks and nuns." She punched Bevyn playfully in the arm. "How did you find out?"

"Apparently, she spent some time in COBU, where she became a novitiate, which is like a nun. The best part is that Bob was the leader!"

Jennifer stared at the Persian carpet in the middle of the room. She put her finger to her lips and then snapped her fingers. "I think I remember. She sent me a letter that I forgot about. It mentioned that she had joined a group, but was seriously concerned about the leader. She claimed he was taking liberties with some of the younger female recruits."

Bevyn went to the window and weighed the police detective's information. "She switched to reporting, interestingly enough. But more importantly, we have a connection between Bob and her. I wonder if she had a score to settle."

Outdoors, squirrels surrounded the fountain, busily gathering peanuts someone had tossed on the grass. The parking lot remained full. An SQ patrol car had taken up a post at the entrance, stopping anyone entering or leaving the retreat.

"What about the basement?"

Bevyn spun around on his heels. "They questioned Brent, but he hasn't a clue what we're talking about. His partner, Ivan somehow gave us the slip. He's headed back though, heeding some strong advice from the Montreal police."

"Any news on Caroline's looking into the death threats over the hidden treasure?"

"Nada." Bevyn started to pace. "Jay, my reporter friend couldn't add anything either."

A random memory of his initiation into the Order flitted through Bevyn's brain all of a sudden; the past influencing the present. The difficulty of overcoming and distancing oneself from one's past was real, but not a sentence. He came back to the topic of conversation.

"Can't imagine why they would be looking for treasure here," Bevyn noted.

"Do you think Dom Chevalier is involved somehow?"

Bevyn reflected on his relationship past and present with the dom. He shared a story involving Chevalier and his old sensei. Jennifer listened without comment, fully aware of the challenges of the personal life impacting the professional.

Bevyn changed the topic mid-sentence. "Back to Caroline. We know she was working on an article about The Secret treasure hunters and maybe something to do with Bob. Also, she met a weirdo in a twelve-step group, and was briefly a sort of nun."

"The first two could be related, but the third. . . . Why did you change the subject?"

"I'm following a thread. I just don't get the green dress part. The man recognized her in it."

"Anything in her diary?" Bevyn said.

"I almost forgot about it! I was going through it again

yesterday looking for clues, when I came across a poem she wrote in the spring of this year."

Jennifer removed the diary from her purse. With the wind picking up and leaves hitting the window panes, she read the poem aloud.

Healing

*There's a way
you must learn to feel
Again
Be who you were denied
and deny who you were
so, you may grow
flower stunted but alive
surely die
so, a new creation
From the scattered seeds
can flourish
so, with care, watering and Love
there will be rebirth
a new life
restored to sanity
filled with joy for life
long awaited
finally living Grace.*

Silence fell between them. A couple ambled by the window hand-in-hand, and a dog ran past followed by its master, a woman in her twenties dressed like a Paris model. Bevyn pointed to the parade of characters outside.

Jennifer waved her hand in the air. "Let's stay in the moment," she remarked and went back to the poem. "Poor Caroline. If I'd only known. Maybe something happened in the cult."

The dog sped past the window, running after a ball. Bevyn went to the window ledge and grinned at the dog's antics. "What did you dig up on the Clint?"

"Pot dealing, possession, a couple of traffic violations and his most recent speeding ticket. Nothing out of character, but nothing suggesting he's capable of murder."

Bevyn picked up a cushion with the names of famous authors, such as Poe, Holmes, Queen and James embroidered on it. "Did you talk to the patrol officer who stopped him for speeding?"

"I did, and he reported nothing unusual about Clint that day."

They were weighing the significance of the infraction when Jennifer spotted two men walking along the edge of the lake with wireless headsets. The hairs on the back of Bevyn's arm stood on end. There was no mistaking that they were hunting for the two investigators.

The professor motioned to an exit, and they left the parlour in haste. They moved along the corridor until they reached the ballroom. They halted. Two gangster costumes lay on the back of a chair. Bevyn grabbed one and handed one to Jennifer. They slipped into a nearby alcove and donned the black suits from the '40s. Fedoras conveniently hung on hooks nearby, and they slipped them on, pulling the brims low over their eyes.

They went back to the ballroom and took up seats near an emergency exit. Two of Poncho's henchmen entered and scanned the crowd. The impossibility of their task must have hit them because the burlier of the two started speaking into his headset. The dialogue lasted only a few seconds. The two men left, trailed by two plainclothes officers dressed as waiters.

Everyone fell silent when Bob stepped up to the microphone in the ball room. He adjusted the bowtie on his tuxedo and fiddled with the cuffs on his suit before launching into his best rendition of a man in complete control. "Ladies and gentlemen, at midnight we will announce our killer!"

Faint and spotty applause resulted. Not pleased and determined, Bob upped the ante. "Ladies and gentlemen, to compensate for the weekend's inconveniences, we at the Bakerstreet have upped the prize money to $25,000. And we've added a second-place prize of $10,000!"

The applause increased a few decibels, and a grin spread across Bob's lips. He smiled at one of his men standing to the side of the raised platform. The crowd went quiet.

"We have a local celebrity with us tonight. He's known for helping the police from time to time as an amateur sleuth. We know him as a professor of English literature at the university, and he's been participating in the events at Bakerstreet. He'll now share a few tips about solving our murder. Please help me welcome Professor Bevyn Jones."

Bevyn remained glued to the spot, stunned by the introduction and request. Bob had forgotten to inform him. The mystery retreat participants applauded, looking around for the special guest. When Bevyn didn't appear, the crowd grew restless and nervous. Not wanting to disappoint them, Bevyn put on his best demeanour and waved his hand. The applause resumed and reached a crescendo as he approached the platform at the front of the room. Bob shook his hand and whispered in his ear. "Jones, you're out of uniform."

Bevyn stepped up to the microphone and fought the urge to insult the manager publicly. Bob joined his man at the side of the stage. The applause died down. Bevyn continued where Bob left off. "Master sleuths, we have a complicated case before us and I want to personally thank you for cooperating with the police."

The crowd exploded in chatter. Bevyn waited until it died down. "We know that the lady in the boathouse danced here Friday night and that many of you saw her with a caped man."

Many in the crowd exchanged puzzled glances. Jennifer smiled when she realized what Bevyn was doing.

"The murderer is close to being caught," he announced.

The room broke out into a beehive of suspicion. Bob slid over to Bevyn. "What are you doing, Jones?"

"What? Didn't you say you'd announce the killer tonight?"

"Yes, but, it's just a marketing tactic," Bob said and withdrew despite his perturbation.

Bevyn continued. "As you all know, a woman's body was found in the boathouse. Autopsy results reveal the cause of death to be a blow to the head. What we don't know is who would kill an innocent woman. By tonight I will tell you!"

A lady in the front row let out a cry and someone grabbed her as she swooned. Bevyn stepped away from the microphone and left the platform, grabbing Jennifer on his way out the emergency exit. He heard Bob's pleas for calm as the door slammed shut.

Moments later, they whisked along the emergency stairway upwards to the mansion's top floor. He whistled a Broadway tune from *Annie* as they went. Jennifer tried to keep up the pace. "Do you think it'll flush the killer out?"

Bevyn stopped for a second. "Definitely." He looked at his smart phone. "We don't have much time, because of Bob's theatrics back there."

Jennifer noticed her partner's hesitation and inquired as to why.

"There's someone I'd like you to get reacquainted with."

Bevyn marched down a series of corridors configured like catacombs until they reached a narrow staircase. They climbed rickety steps to the attic. A short and narrow hallway opened to a small chapel located at the extreme north end of the mansion. A votive candle lit the sanctuary, and shadows danced on the ceiling. A simple altar with a few Eastern Orthodox icons covered the front wall. The air smelled of dust and old varnish, and wilted flowers hung limp in vases placed in diametrically opposed recessed panels.

"Well, this is your show. Can you tell me why we are here?"

Bevyn held a finger to his lips. They sat down. The chapel was stuffy and cramped. She heard leaves on the slate roof outside, and, despite the sun, a slight draft made Jennifer shiver. She smelled the candle wax and noticed the icon for the first time. Religious figures did nothing for her.

"Can't picture you as a monk, Bevyn."

He leaned over like he was praying. "It's a life of devotion and service." Bevyn lifted his nose high in the air. "It had its moments."

"What changed?"

Bevyn's muted laugh sounded hollow in the small space. "A series of events that led me to the conclusion that I was trying to escape life." He felt a pang of nostalgia, but otherwise, nothing else over the admission, but he still felt regret for having wasted so much valuable time, even though he understood that everyone did the same at some point in their lives.

Jennifer heard the sound of steps approaching from behind. Alarmed, she swivelled her head around and saw Caroline walking toward them like a ghost. Flabbergasted, Jennifer stifled a shriek, more out of relief than shock, rushed to her friend, and wrapped her arms around her. The former coeds held each other for a minute. Jennifer gave Bevyn a rueful gaze. Caroline saw it. "I swore him to secrecy. He wanted to tell you from the start, but Murphy wouldn't have it."

"He told me the whole story about the death threats and about Beth. I thought you were holed up somewhere. What are you doing here?"

Caroline answered Jennifer's questions with succinctness. "It was a case of mistaken identity. I substituted my costume with her that night. Whoever killed her expected me to be in it. Bevyn wanted to talk about that night, so I agreed to meet here."

"I don't understand. Wouldn't a phone call be wiser?"

Caroline's lips trembled. "A woman died instead of me. I want to help find her killer."

"But what happened? Who is after you? Have you been in the loop about Brent and our findings? What about your own research for your story?"

Jennifer cleared her throat and whispered. "It's not important. I wanted you to know, but I couldn't risk anyone close to me getting involved, except my mother."

Jennifer diverted her attention to Bevyn. "Anyone at the mansion know about this?"

"Bob isn't in the loop, but I think he suspects something."

Caroline sat down and exhaled deeply. "I think it's because of the story about the The Secret. Brent and Ivan don't want anyone else on the trail. People say they are threatening other treasure hunters."

Jennifer gazed into Caroline's eyes. "What about the super, Clint?"

"Oh, he's creepy, but I never thought of him as being involved in this mess."

Bevyn interjected. "We visited with him. He had a peculiar obsession with our victim. Do you know anything about that?"

Caroline sneezed over the stale air wafting inside her nostrils. "We exchanged dresses, and that's about it. Horrible what happened to her. Who would do such a thing?"

Jennifer brought her hand to her head. "What happened on

Friday night?"

"Nothing. I danced with Brent to try and seduce some more information out of him." She winked.

A thought popped into Jennifer's head. "Why did you change the dress?"

Caroline's lips drew to a thin line. "I hated that thing! Poor Beth thought it was fabulous. I would trade places with her in a heartbeat!

Bevyn and Jennifer exchanged glances. The policewoman could tell from the slight downward curve in Bevyn's lower lip that he wasn't buying the reporter's story.

"So, it was you in the room with Bell," Bevyn said. He added, "What story were you doing on Bob? We learned that you spent time at a commune where he was the leader."

Caroline considered her answer before responding. "Oh, it was just about the murder mystery business, you know . . ." She stifled a sneeze before continuing. "Anyway . . ." Her face screwed up as she struggled to get out her words. "I walked in. There Bell was on the floor."

Caroline's admission piqued Jennifer's suspicion.

"And no one knew who you were, and you were wearing a costume, no doubt," Jennifer said.

"Yes, dressed as a butler that day. I used the passageway, of course."

Jennifer went into detective mode. "If I get this straight, you plan to ask Bell about Bob's activities. You meet him in the room. You arrive and find him dead. You exit by the passageway. You take the motorboat and beach it. It occurs to you that two people are dead, one of whom is supposed to be you for reasons you don't understand. But how did the boat get back, and why didn't you just meet Bell in the ballroom? Why the secrecy?"

"Okay, shit . . . Bob's a crook and Bell had some information on him. He insisted we meet somewhere secret. It's only later that I put two and two together. The black dress, the boathouse, the note . . . As for the boat, I don't know what happened to it."

Bevyn's ears pricked up. "What note? Put what together?"

"One of the hospitality crew gave it to her. It was intended for me. I found it on the floor. She must have accidentally dropped it. I totally forgot about it," Caroline said.

Bevyn stood up and approached the icon of Jesus on the wall. The Christ figure hung on a Taize cross, five feet tall and brightly coloured in red. As he studied the work, he digested Caroline's information.

Jennifer blinked a few times while shaking her head. "You had a note, and you forgot to tell the police?"

Caroline nodded sheepishly.

"What did the note say?"

"Meet me at the boathouse at 11:00."

"And you went that late, alone?"

"Why not? There were people outside on the grounds."

Bevyn faced Caroline from across the sanctuary, his face dark. "I'll tell you what happened. You went to the boathouse to meet the woman and you killed her. There never was any note!"

Jennifer jumped out of her pew even though the thought had crossed her mind already. Caroline launched into staccato laughter.

"I went there, yes, but the boathouse was empty. Why would I kill her? I have no motive. I met Beth in a twelve-step group I was investigating. She called herself Nicole. The last place I expected to see her was here!"

"We know about the group. Maybe she had something to tell you about Clint?"

Jennifer watched Bevyn out of the corner of her eye.

Caroline shook her head, mystified. "I have no idea why she was here. I saw her a few times when I was in the group investigating my story, and I exchanged dresses with her. *Point final.*"

"Where's the note now?"

Caroline rummaged through her pockets.

"Well?" Bevyn remarked.

She shrugged her shoulders. "Huh, I must have left it somewhere."

Jennifer intervened on her friend's behalf. "It doesn't matter. You panicked. Who would call her to the boathouse late at night? Clint?"

Jennifer knew her friend well enough to know even after all the years that had passed that she was lying when she responded by shaking her head.

Bevyn let out a large exhale of breath, his brow furrowed with deep crevices. "What do you think Bell was going to say?"

"I think he wanted to confirm my suspicions about Bob. The Bakerstreet manager was into illegal activities, gambling and fraud. The same kind of stuff he dallied with at the commune."

Bevyn felt a knot in his shoulder. A nativity scene carved in wood sat on a table inside a glass cube at the back of the chapel. He ambled up to it and told Caroline over his shoulder that Bell died of a heart attack. She didn't react.

No one spoke for a while. The sound of distant footsteps climbing the stairs halted the questioning. Caroline broke the silence first with a shrug.

"Like I told Bevyn, I have gone over and over it. I dunno, but I think someone wanted me dead, either Bob or maybe even Brent and Ivan."

They felt the movement of air as the wind gusted and whistled through the walls. A dry, wrinkled leaf rolled across the floor and came to rest at Bevyn's feet. "Is there anything else you haven't told us?"

Caroline paused and slowly shook her head. "I really, really forgot about the note. I was terrified of being killed, don't you get it?"

Bevyn grunted. "Oh, I get it all right. And now, I think we better leave. We have company." He placed his hand on Jennifer's shoulder.

"One last question. Did you see Beth with anyone, anyone at all?" Jennifer asked.

Bevyn picked up the leaf and twirled it by the stem between his thumb and first finger. He looked at the women. He adjusted the collar of his wool coat.

Caroline cried, "Don't you believe me?"

Bevyn ran his tongue around the inside of his mouth and he laughed cynically. Jennifer wore a stone face and Caroline's was crestfallen. Footsteps reached the top of the stairs and stopped. It was time to vacate the premises.

The women followed Bevyn to the altar, where he reached into a recess with his hand, and a secret door hissed open. They dashed through the door, and it closed behind them without a sound. After a steep descent down a spiral staircase that changed directions halfway from clockwise to counter-clockwise, they arrived at the main floor. Bevyn guided them through the solarium, and then he veered left down a long hallway with windows overlooking the distant lake. An egress at the end of the corridor led outside. The smell of leaves and fresh-cut grass hit their nostrils, a welcome relief from the musty smell of the chapel.

They followed a well-worn path in the woods. It twisted and weaved until they reached a dark section that branched off the path completely. They stopped after a few minutes to catch their breaths. Caroline leaned against a tree. Jennifer and Bevyn cocked their ears for sounds of pursuit.

They looked over a fence and saw a small cemetery: bone-white tombstones, names, dates, and epitaphs worn with age. Bevyn stepped through a metal archway and followed ruts in the grass. The wind lightly rustled the remaining leaves clinging to the trees.

"What are we doing here?" Caroline whispered.

Bevyn stopped and looked behind. "I think maybe I'm getting paranoid, but I'm not taking any chances after my dip in the lake."

"Let's just keeping moving. This place gives me the creeps," Jennifer murmured, keeping her head low as if bats were going to swoop down and land in her hair.

Bevyn looked at the moon to get his bearings, and the women fell into step. Caroline followed last. They arrived at a promontory overlooking the mansion and halted to catch their breath. A few people strolled outside in the late afternoon. They reached the gardens, the lights from the dining room ablaze.

Bevyn hesitated outside the pool house door before inserting the key in the lock. He pushed the door inward, and the three filed in. Bevyn warned them to leave the lights off. The women sat on the sectional sofa. Bevyn went to the window and pulled aside the drapes to check outside.

Jennifer sat back and placed her arm along the back of the sofa, while her friend picked up a cushion and hugged it. They sat in silence until the detective broke the silence.

"What led you back to Bob, Caroline?"

"I dunno. Curiosity, I guess. He always managed to escape

the law and I wondered if I could find something on him this time." Caroline picked up a magazine on the coffee table, flipped through a few pages and tossed it back.

The clouds had overtaken the sky, and a few raindrops fell on the metal roof. A group of people came up the path and passed by the pool house.

A ladybug landed on Bevyn's shoulder. He watched its wings fold under its retracting shell. It stayed for few seconds and flew off. He had read somewhere that a ladybug lived thirty days. Caroline put her feet up on the coffee table and tossed her head back in boredom.

"What do you know about Ivan?" Jennifer said.

Caroline shrugged her shoulders. "I got nothing from him. I asked him about the threats over The Secret's hidden treasure. He told me he wasn't worried for his safety; they weren't going to stop him."

"Brent said you had a thing for him."

Caroline burst out laughing. "What a joke! He's totally deluded—a total creep. Honestly of all the things to say!"

Bevyn left the window and joined the women on the sofa. He shared a rueful grin with Jennifer, aware people close to them had secrets they were unwilling to share. He had a conviction about Peters all of a sudden. He accepted that the old monk who had been like a parent to him for most of his adult life, had secrets. Bevyn needed to knock the old religious man off the pedestal, and he sensed Peters longed to get something off his chest.

The wind picked up, and lilac tree branches scratched against the side of the building. Bevyn checked his smart phone. Ladybug had broken her silence, ruling out Caroline as the sender.

```
Ladybug has left her shell.
```

He took another quick look at the screen without arousing suspicion. He wondered more and more about the connection between Clint, Beth, and Caroline outside the support group and whether something had gone terribly wrong between them, leading to Beth's death. Even more relevant, was Bob's dealings and the numbers that he had downloaded off the manager's computer. Lastly, did Ivan and Brent threaten Caroline's life? Was it a case of mistaken identity? He had to find out soon. Caroline wasn't going to tell the whole story unless he could catch her off guard and the window of opportunity was closing fast.

Chapter XVI

Roy and Murphy sat in the chief's office reviewing a videotape of the stranger in the blue van. The sound system in the squad room played "achy-breaky-heart muzak" from a Vermont FM radio station. The two men bantered back and forth, talking aloud. It was a typical day in the life of a small-town police station with an atypical case to solve.

They studied the tape of the loading area behind the police station, but there was nothing unusual to see. The plant guy parked his van and entered the building and later left with a dead fern and a coffee cup he had brought with him.

Roy stopped the tape and Murphy grunted. The chief picked up a file lying on his desk and opened it.

"Clint has had quite the heartbreaker of a life. Abusive father, depressed mother, bullying, taxing, yadda yadda. He should be a regular axe murderer." The phone rang. He uttered a few monosyllables and hung up. "We got a monk missing at the monastery."

"A missing monk. *Ostie, c'est la fin du monde!*"

"I told them you'd pay them a visit again."

Roy rubbed his eyes. "Maybe they talk this time, especially that Peters monk. But one monk . . ." He pulled out his notebook. "*Un Anglais*, Kirk, tell me a little until Chevalier show up." He gave the video one last glance. "What about van?"

"Send the New Guy to follow up."

"No problem, Chief." Roy arose to leave.

Murphy glanced at the folder and picked up the phone receiver and waved it at Roy. "How are things going with Bentley's family?"

"Family upset we keep it secret, but happy we work on case. They want person who kill their daughter." Roy sucked on his lower lip and left.

Murphy dialled while he tidied his desktop. The phone rang for a while until Bevyn answered. He listened briefly before yapping.

"Can't talk long, yeppers . . . Hinges does have a two-hour window of unaccountable time. Yeppers, no, dunno. . . . No worries. We released Bentley to the family today. Very sad. Stay low. The SQ still considers you a person of interest."

He hung up and peered at the clock on his desk. He wondered what Beth had done, if anything, to deserve a whack on the head. Was it a case of mistaken identity because of the dress swap? Crime of passion? Information? Blackmail? He crossed out the last one in his head; Bentley didn't seem the kind of girl. But these days, one couldn't be sure of anything.

The New Guy passed by the door opening. Murphy called him into the office. The bright, fresh face briefly picked up the chief's spirits. "Officer Morrison, please bring the car around for me and Roy."

"Sure, but can I finish my panini first?"

"Your what?" The chief slid his thumb and first finger up and down one of his suspenders. The kid pointed at the bread in his hand. Murphy saw the crumbs on the officer's chin and stifled a remark. "Bring the patrol car around."

"Can I finish eating?"

"It's an order, son." Murphy stared at the ceiling and back at the young officer, critical of the current generation of recruits.

The New Guy remained glued to the spot, dumbfounded by

his superior's words, wondering if the chief was undermining his rights. In the interests of job promotion, he heeded his superior's order and grabbed his coat off the coat tree, keeping his lunch intact.

Jennifer and Caroline waited in the living room while Bevyn called Jay from the bedroom. He had given the reporter an undercover job to find out more about Caroline's assignments. He answered the phone. A long pause followed an exclamation of disgust.

"I found out Caroline had some gambling problems."

Bevyn spoke his thoughts aloud. "She wasn't doing a story on Bakerstreet then, she was begging for mercy from Bob." He sighed. "What else?"

Jay requested that Bevyn explain his last remark. Jennifer watched Bevyn through the open door. He put his back to her.

"I'll explain later. What about her other assignments?"

Jay continued with a litany of facts about the roving reporter and her latest adventures in journalism, ending with a riff on 12-twelve groups.

"Jay, just the facts, please. What about The Secret and the treasure hunters?"

Jay didn't reply. Static on the line caused Bevyn to draw the smart phone away from his ear. When the line cleared up, the reporter admitted that he hadn't found anything relevant yet. Before they could sign off, the signal strength dropped again, and the line went dead.

Bevyn considered the information before returning to Jennifer and Caroline.

"Is everything alright, Bevyn? You look a little white," Jennifer asked, jutting her chin out a little in a less than attractive manner. "Are you going to tell me what's going on?"

Caroline rose to her feet and joined Jennifer in the inquisition, albeit more out of curiosity.

"Nothing to worry about. All under control."

"When someone says that, it usually isn't," Caroline said.

Bevyn volunteered no more and went back to the window. Caroline put her hands up. "I can't stay here forever."

"She's right, Bevyn."

Bevyn dropped the curtains back across the window and

looked at the women. "I am open to ideas."

"You always say that and don't really mean it," Jennifer replied.

He took a large step over to the fireplace and picked up a poker and played with the ashes in the hearth. Caroline watched him with her hands on her hips, and Jennifer remained still with her palms facing the ceiling. Caroline tapped her foot.

After a brief period of reflection, Bevyn replaced the poker. He strode to the door and exited the pool house. The air was damp, and he heard rustling sounds in the woods. An owl hooted somewhere in the distance. Bevyn saw the outline of the mansion through the naked trees.

A very loud thunderclap rattled the windows, and a flash of lightning lit up the sky. The women, antsy over the inaction, crossed their arms. Jennifer sneezed as a few drops of rain fell. She wrapped her coat tighter around her body.

Bevyn returned inside and saw the resolve in Caroline's face. He knew she wasn't going to hang around any longer. He resisted the urge to stop her. Seconds later, Caroline threw up her hands in disgust.

"I can't do this any longer," she said and crossed the room and banged out the door, leaving it open behind her.

Bevyn reached into his pocket and removed two power bars. He handed one to Jennifer and ripped open the wrapper on the other.

"Puh-leeze. I'm not hungry. Jennifer said as she gazed at the bar in her hand with contempt, but then tore open the wrapper, and gobbled it down.

A few moments later, the rain subsided. They gazed through the large picture window overlooking the lake. An ethereal mist rose off its surface. Jennifer heard a muffled thud. "Did you hear that?"

Bevyn put a finger to his lips. Jennifer removed her gun from her holster and edged her way along the wall toward the back door. She pointed toward the main door and Bevyn nodded.

The building shook to a long roll of thunder. There was a crash at the back door and a scuffle. Seconds later, she heard the sound of body blows at the front door.

A moment later, Bevyn dragged a half-conscious man in a

black sweater into the room and threw him on the floor. Jennifer emerged, pointing a gun at another man. A policeman entered the front door, gun drawn. Jennifer whipped out her badge. The officer looked confused until two other officers entered the back door, one of whom took charge.

"Bring everybody here," Gervais ordered.

Two officers relieved Bevyn and Jennifer of the intruders and cuffed them. Not long after, another officer entered the cottage with a very fat man.

Poncho gave Jennifer a contemptuous grin. An officer nudged him toward a chair while covering him with his weapon.

"We never seem to find time alone. I thought you were dead, Jenn."

The Commanding Officer came up to Bevyn and grabbed him by the arm. Bevyn restrained his instinct to react. Gervais patted him down.

"What's the meaning of this?" Jennifer's face was already flushed with exertion and it turned redder.

"M. Jones is under arrest," Gervais announced.

"On what grounds?"

The CO's face hardened. One of the gorillas groaned and slumped to the floor. The cop bent down to tend to him. Poncho saw his chance and ran for the rear door.

"He's getting away!" Jennifer cried.

Poncho tried to hop over the railing but caught his foot on the top banister. The whole thing came crashing down on top of him. Winded, he gave little resistance to the policemen converging on him.

The CO couldn't help chuckling. He diverted his attention to Bevyn and spoke a few guttural words in French. "You have a lot of explaining to do, Mr. Jones."

Murphy and Roy, siren blaring, pulled up behind the SQ patrol cars. Murphy, despite an inner tube wobbling around his mid-section, dashed to the house. He ran right past Bevyn and the CO.

Gervais watched the antics with mirth. He called out to the chief. Murphy did a double-take and halted. The CO gave the head of the local police department time to catch his breath. Next, he faced his English-speaking colleague and with a touch of condescension, remarked, "You have no jurisdiction, *mon ami*. Heez under arrest."

"On what charge?" Murphy stammered.

"Obstruction of justice and accessory to murder."

Bevyn, regrouping after taking out the ruffian, tipped his hat at Murphy. "Good to see you, old sport. You missed all the fun."

"Yeah, well, Roy had to stop for donuts on the way."

Gervais cleared his voice and hollered instructions in French to his men. Murphy waited until the CO finished and then took him aside. They talked a few moments. After raised voices and a few grunts of assent, Murphy went to Bevyn, took him by the arm, and produced handcuffs.

"Sorry, Jones, I can take you in, but on condition."

"Charmed."

"Don't worry. They got nothing on you."

"I *know*, Chief."

Murphy didn't catch the inflection in Bevyn's voice, but Roy's ears picked it up, Jennifer let out a cry, and Caroline stared at Bevyn in disbelief. The CO shouted more orders at his men.

"You mean," Jennifer said, adjusting the holster around her torso. "You know the killer!"

Bevyn gave a wry smile like a little kid after his first kiss with the girl-next-door. "All in good time, all in good time. But first, a trip to police headquarters for some old-time rubber hoses."

The Hells Angels, SQ officers, police, and civilians filed into vehicles and drove off in a parade of lights, leaving cancerous automobile exhaust hanging in the air.

After some time, silence descended over Bakerstreet mansion's grounds and woods. Wary deer peered from behind trees, their noses twitching in the air as they checked for the presence of human scents. The moon appeared from behind the lingering clouds, giving the foliage an infrared-like cast. Somewhere down the lake, a loon loosed a mournful cry.

Chapter XVII

The natural daylight filtering through the drapes blended nicely with the light cast by converted braziers. The marquee flooring shone like glass, and dark oak panelling on the walls glistened. On each side of the main door, police officers stood like statues, clasping their belt buckles. The room's sparse furnishings had been pushed to the walls, and folding chairs had been brought in for the Bakerstreet Murder Mystery Retreat's denouement.

A collection of notable people sat near the front, anxious for the proceedings to commence: Victor the California surfer/server, Brent and Ivan, Williams, Mr. Holt and his wife, the nurse, and Isabelle, along with the other retreat participants in the back. Murphy and an officer took positions behind the crowd. Bob sat with Mack, Reuben, and Olivia. Bob's other gorilla stood near a side door. Gervais stood near the front, keeping an eye on Bob and his cohorts. A couple of Gervais' plain-clothed men sat in the crowd. Roy hung around the shadows at the back of the room.

Jennifer and Caroline entered together and sat down. Caroline's appearance brought a gasp from Reuben and Bob. She, in turn, froze momentarily at the sight of Bob. Olivia flicked something off her shoulder, nonplussed. Bevyn stood at the front of the room, leaning on the mantle. The CO silenced the crowd with a wolf whistle, and he prompted Bevyn to begin with a curt nod.

Bevyn moved to the front of the room and cleared his throat. "Thank you for all being here. I know you want to return home as soon as possible."

The assembly murmured in assent, but most sat with strained expressions on their faces. Bevyn's eyes shone, revealing the pleasure he got from a conundrum's resolution.

"I admit, at first this case bedevilled me a great deal. There seemed to be no logic and nothing to tie everything together. Caroline's alive. Sorry for the shock. She's been in hiding. What we don't know is the name of the killer and the name of the woman in the boathouse."

Bob sighed audibly. A few people concurred with his displeasure; others showed anger at the interruption. Bevyn thought it best not to ignore him.

"Have you something to say, Mr. Burton?"

"Will this take long? I need to attend to some matters."

Bevyn licked his lips and gave the manager a big smile. "The garbage can wait to go out." The crowd laughed, and Mack cracked his knuckles. The other gorilla remained still, his hands clasped in front of him. Bob bared his teeth in an attempt at good humour.

Bevyn gulped water from a glass on a table. "There are many threads in this tapestry, but let's start with the boathouse." He paused to survey the crowd. "I knew of the unsolved case in the boathouse. What is the likelihood of lightning striking twice in the same spot? It caused me a great deal of struggle until I realized that the murders were not connected. In fact, the latest murder occurred elsewhere."

The crowd members began to talk amongst themselves. Roy stepped from behind a curtain. "The first was murder? How comes?"

A few people echoed Roy's confusion. Murphy started to stand, but Bevyn cut through the chaos with a large wave of his hand. "Ladies and gentlemen, I need your cooperation if we're to get to the end of this, please. And then you can go home."

The crowd settled down, and Murphy went back in his seat, giving Roy a stare. The CO, Gervais, took out his cell and checked the time. "*Dépechez-vous, Monsieur Jones.*"

Jennifer gave Bevyn a thumb up, and he continued his preamble. "As some of you know, Roy's referring to the death some years ago of local businessman John Peters. The death took place in the boathouse. I can say there's no connection between the two deaths other than a twisted sense of love."

The energy and enthusiasm in the room picked up. Bevyn sauntered over to a corner of the room. "Beth Bentley was the woman found dead in the boathouse. A beautiful girl with black hair and blue eyes. She was a teacher and worked children. Her murderer killed her elsewhere, probably just outside the boathouse. We don't know."

The crowd remained silent, stunned by the news.

"Wonderful woman," Reuben acknowledged.

"I remember her. She was lively and vivacious," Bob remarked wistfully, resulting in hateful stares from some of the women present.

"Why not in the boathouse?" Reuben said.

Bevyn went over to the wall where a large rowboat oar leaned against the brick. He brought it forward and swung it in an arc through the air. The people sitting in the front row drew back, while the rest of the crowd gasped as the oar sliced through the air.

"This is the oar used to kill Beth. It would need a great deal of force and space to do the damage. One can barely stand in the boathouse, let alone swing an oar of this length."

"Maybe another instrument was used," Reuben remarked.

"No, Murphy's men found her blood on the oar all right." Bevyn leaned the oar against the wall. "As I said, she was killed either on the water or elsewhere. It doesn't matter. The important thing is that the murderer made a mistake."

"How so?" Bob interrupted.

"Because someone saw it."

Some people started chatting again, while others looked around nervously.

"Who?" Bob said.

"In due time. Let's back up a bit. The question is what or who drew her away from the party?"

"She arranged to meet someone?" Olivia said.

"But why did she go at such a late hour willingly, even excitedly?"

The imaginations of the women perked up over the possibilities, while the men shook their heads. Bob stood up. "Bevyn, we don't have all day. Some inbred townie probably whacked her like a dog."

A number of people mumbled assent. Others erupted in protest over Bob's word choice. Bevyn pressed onward, ignoring Bob's comment.

"Did Beth know her killer? We don't know, but she *expected* someone. Caroline says there was a note, but what happened to it? She doesn't know. She admitted that she changed costumes with Beth because she hated the Goth look. The question is, was it a case of mistaken identity?"

Murphy and his men scoped the crowd as Bevyn's statement sank in. Roy slid over to a window and drew the drapes aside to peer outside on the cloudy day.

"One thing that always intrigued me was why I was summoned to this place. Was it just coincidence that a murder happened while I was here?"

Roy addressed Bevyn with a stunned face, a toothpick dangling from his lips. "Maybe the person want to make you idiot."

Bevyn laughed good-naturally. "Exactly, *mon ami*. I was the patsy to draw attention elsewhere, like smoke and mirrors. The 'idiot,' as you say."

Roy made a rude sound with his mouth, delighted by his insight, but mistrustful of Bevyn's good nature, the bane of the cynic.

Bevyn took another swig of water. "Let's say the murderer wanted to bring me into the narrative. What kind of person does that kind of thing? It takes cunning and incredibly delicate manipulation and premeditation. Let's look at the facts. The murder occurred early in the morning on Saturday, according to the autopsy. The super checked the boathouse the night before. He stated everything was fine. He found the door open at 7:00, and the body inside. The body was unclothed—"

A few women shouted protests. Bob yelled out over the din

in defence of women everywhere. "The women should have been informed!"

His exclamation further incensed the crowd until Murphy came to Bevyn's aid. "The ladies were never in any danger. Now everyone, keep a lid on it!"

Several guests muttered under their breaths. Jennifer withdrew her smart phone from her pocket and checked the screen. She gave Bevyn a slight nod, which Bevyn acknowledged. Bevyn thanked Murphy for his help with a bow and returned to the mantle, stalling for time.

"Then there's the case of Johnny Bell, whose identity, thanks to the SQ Communications Department and the media, is a well-documented fact. Were there two murders and two murderers and a link between them? I can say 'sort of' and 'yes.'"

"How can a person be killed 'sort of'? He is murdered or not," Gervais asked.

"Jones, *on n'est pas stupide*," Detective Roy muttered.

"Let's clear this up right away, then. Johnny Bell had information for Caroline, but he also had a secret. We'll never know for sure, but I suspect he saw Beth's murder. In any case, Mr. Bell met someone in the room where he was found dead by Caroline. However, why would he meet the killer? It occurred to me that more than one person might be involved in this case."

Some people shuffled uneasily in their seats. Bevyn took a quick look at the rear door. He looked at Jennifer, who raised her eyes to the ceiling and screwed up her mouth. Murphy coughed and flashed five fingers on his right hand twice.

"Poor Mr. Bell had a preexisting heart condition. Whoever met him probably wanted to threaten him first, and, if that didn't work, then kill him. Caroline found him dead of a heart attack, brought on by the stress of the encounter—a 'sort of' murder. Evil in intent, but not, legally speaking, a murder."

"Why didn't he go to the police right away?" Reuben asked.

"I suspect blackmail was on his mind. He owed large sums of money to someone in this room."

"To whom?" Olivia said.

The thought passed through Bevyn's mind that Bell's choices led to his demise. Despite the thought, he could not but share in lifting the crowd's spirits that had been heavy since the beginning of the proceedings. The realization hit him that the light he had been looking for at the end of the proverbial tunnel was around the corner.

"And the other . . . what you call?" Gervais asked.

"That's where things get complicated."

Bevyn stared at the crowd. The oar slid across the wall and hit the floor with a loud bang. Everyone jumped. The professor started to pace the front of the room. "When we found out about the costume change, Murphy and I—"

Roy grunted.

"And *Roy* believed Beth had not been the intended victim. But if that were so, where was Caroline, what on earth happened to Beth's clothes, and why was she nude? There was no sign of sexual assault."

Bevyn reached into a garbage bag that had been sitting in a corner, attracting the attention of many since the evening began. He produced a black costume and held it up for the audience. He jiggled it and let it sway in Caroline's direction. "Is this the costume you gave Beth?"

She gave the costume a once over. "I believe so."

"Come have a look."

Caroline stroked her upper left arm with her right hand. "No, that's okay. I am sure that's it."

"I insist."

Caroline took a few paces toward Bevyn and nodded an affirmative.

"Are you sure?"

Caroline shouted, "Yes!" and sat down in her chair in a huff.

"We found no sign of blood on the costume. But make a note that it was in fact the one worn by Caroline and Beth. We'll come back to it."

Caroline swore out loud, getting everyone's attention.

"But how is that possible?" Olivia asked.

"You said yourself that she was found nude," Bob remarked.

"Oh, it *is* a case of mistaken identity," Bevyn declared.

Caroline riveted her eyes on the black dress in Bevyn's

hands. Her left eye developed a twitch.

"You are speaking in riddles," Bob said sarcastically.

"My friends, Beth went to the boathouse. The killer was waiting to take her on the ride of her life. She wore the costume hoping to give her lover a surprise."

The women in the crowd nodded to each other in quiet confirmation of their suspicions, and the men shook their heads in complete disgust over the revelation. Gervais let out another wolf whistle to calm things down.

"Where was the black dress found then?" Reuben inquired.

"We'll come to that in a minute."

The crowd went silent as a funeral procession.

"We decided to play along with the murderer and let him believe he had killed Caroline. But what we didn't realize was that Beth had been the intended victim all along."

The lights on the wall flickered when a member of the staff switched on the gas fireplace.

Caroline's jaw dropped. She broke the silence with a question. "Why did I get threatening phone calls?"

Bevyn pranced over to her area of the room, rubbing his hands together like an inventor over a prototype. "Indeed, why did you get the calls?"

The reporter shifted in her chair, while Murphy and Roy moved toward the throng of seated guests and staff.

"You contacted me that day, informing me of your predicament. After conferring with Murphy, we agreed to shield you."

Caroline frowned as the crowd watched. "I had been researching some stories."

"Yes, very interesting stories about Bakerstreet and hidden treasure and threats. But you forgot the one about the 12-Step group. I have a question though. Why the big secrecy? Why didn't you just tell me you feared for your life when you summoned me here for the weekend?"

"I didn't think you'd believe me."

A few people in the room discussed the latest admission. Bevyn paused for the discourse to die down.

"I guess I wasn't thinking straight because I was getting threatening phone calls," Caroline added in chagrin.

"That you deleted."

"They were just too awful." She twisted her hands in anguish.

"I was in the dark for a good long time, but we caught a break when we searched the property for discarded items." Bevyn shook the black dress in his hands. "A few people saw you wearing this."

Caroline waved her hand in the air with quiet assent. "So? The killer whacked her, undressed her, and hid it."

"Who would want to kill Beth?" Reuben remarked.

"Jones, where in hell are you going with all this?" Bob whined.

Gervais gave Bevyn an impatient head bob and Murphy a look of frustration. The amateur sleuth resolved the mounting tension by raising his voice and saying, "Beth's lover realized he'd been had, and because of his background, he could not go to the police. So he sent text messages to me."

"Maybe he arranged for her death?" Bob inquired.

"No, a little DNA test confirmed my suspicion."

"Test for what?" Caroline said.

"Paternity."

"You mean . . ."

"Beth carried the man's child. She was about three months pregnant."

Caroline sank in her chair, her face blank.

"What does it matter whether she was pregnant or not?" Bob said.

Bevyn squared his body to Caroline. "How well do you know the super here, also known as Clint? He's hard to miss with those hinges on his arms."

"He's . . . how dare you bring that into this!"

"He spurned you, did he not?"

A smug smile came to Caroline's lips, and she sat up straighter in her chair like a schoolgirl asserting her dominance. "God, he thought he loved me, pathetic."

"You're not much for rejection, are you Caroline? In fact, you loved him."

Two of Murphy's men edged a little closer to Caroline on the chief's cue.

"He's just some guy I met!"

"He took lots and lots of pictures. At first, Jennifer and I thought maybe he was just another pervert, but he loved Beth."

A thin smile crossed Caroline's mouth. As composed as a panther, she stared at her fingertips like they were claws. "You have no proof."

"Oh, I think Beth can speak for herself. All the way from the grave."

"You're confused, Professor Jones, Beth's dead. And her lover, like most men, is missing in action." A dark smile crossed Caroline's face.

"I suppose he's long gone by now, eh, Caroline?"

"I bet my last loonie."

Right on cue, the main doors opened, and a commotion ensued, reaching everyone's ears. Caroline arose with everyone else to see the source of the interruption. Bevyn gave Murphy a nod. Two husky officers deposited a dishevelled and unshaven Clint, a.k.a., the waterfront supervisor, at the front of the room. Bevyn continued, addressing Caroline.

"Beth was in your twelve-step group. He fell for her, but you couldn't have that, could you? You had her killed and the body placed in the boathouse. You tried to implicate him for some extra assurance."

"Absolutely false! I won't put up with this any longer." She started toward the door when two officers stepped in her path. "Let me pass or I'll sue!"

Clint looked at Caroline. "Is it true? Did you know about the child?"

"They're playing you, Clint, shut up!"

All the blood drained from Clint's face. His face screwed up with rage, but the officers restrained him. He shouted some choice expletives. Meanwhile, the cops took hold of Caroline, who still sought the exit door.

"You got nothing. Arrest him! He did it. I didn't do a thing!" Caroline yelled out at the top of her lungs.

Clint tried to get at Caroline. "Tried to nail me, eh? I showed you by sending texts!"

"Shut up! Shut up! Everything was fine until you fell for that bitch!"

Murphy came over, joined by Gervais who waved at the men. "Get them outta here. I'm getting indigestion listening to them."

Gervais clapped his hands, and the officers dragged Clint out of the room, while two others wrestled with Caroline, who was hollering and screaming, calling for a number of grisly ends for the super and Bevyn. Everyone gawked until Bevyn's voice cut through the noise and confusion. With total command, he asked everyone to sit down and get ready for Act 2. He waited for silence and then he picked up where he had left off.

"A short recap. Clint finds Beth dead. Thinks Caroline might have done it. Caroline throws everyone off with the dress substitution and claims she's in danger. She gets him to shut up by telling him she loves him. Everyone buys it, including Bevyn Jones, a.k.a. Sherlock Holmes."

Roy let out a huge sardonic laugh and saluted Bevyn.

"So, Bevyn, if I get this straight, Caroline killed Beth, claimed she was the intended victim—"

"Caroline didn't kill Beth."

Jennifer's jaw dropped. Olivia spoke up for the first time. "Well, who did it then, Bevyn?"

Bevyn pivoted 180° and directed a question at Bob. "An excellent question. Do you care to answer?"

Bob startled out of his composure, furrowed his brow, and brought his eyebrows together with apprehension. Then, suddenly, his face lightened when all eyes focused on him. He roared with laughter.

"Superb, Jones, superb! What a finale to the weekend!" He got up and ran to the back of the room. Everyone swivelled in their seats. "People, people! We now know who will win the pot! Bevyn Jones!" He clapped and exhorted everyone to join him.

Bevyn raised his voice to a feverish pitch. "What was Johnny Bell going to tell Caroline about? A murder, perhaps? Some gambling action?" The professor's eyes bored into Bob's. "It's so difficult to change our spots and escape the past, isn't that true, Bob?"

"God, Bevyn, you are such an amateur with all this speculation," Bob said.

"Too bad the dress turned up in one of your bins."

"I have no idea what you're talking about. It's not my business if you're into black dresses."

"You like numbers, Bob? I got a lot of them here in neat little rows."

Bevyn held up a sheet of paper with the random numbers copied from Bob's laptop. Meanwhile, Mack joined his boss and the other gorilla at the back of the room. The cops put their hands on their weapons.

"What if I like a little action now and then?"

"The place is surrounded, *Monsieur* Bob. Stop now," Gervais threatened.

"That dress doesn't prove anything. I didn't even know the girl."

"Then why had she been seen leaving your room the night before the murder by a member of the hospitality crew, looking more than a bit flustered?"

Bob reeled over the accusation. His eyes darted to Victor, who was smiling as doleful as a lamb. Bob rallied like a true tennis player. "Jones, you are full of proverbial shit. You got nothing, and you're nothing but an amateurish clod. I have an alibi for that night."

"Of course, you do. That's why you sent Mack to do the job."

Bob sprang into action. He pushed on a wall panel. It opened, and he dashed through. The two gorillas blocked the doorway, but the cops moved in fast. A struggle ensued. The guests watched in fascination as the cops eventually subdued the burly men.

Murphy watched the altercation develop with amusement. He withdrew his walkie-talkie and barked a few words into it. The fugitive's flight faced a short end.

Everyone stood in horror, staring at each other like they had just witnessed a lynching. The police cuffed the two henchmen. A minute later, Murphy's walkie-talkie squawked. He nodded his head and laughed, waving the device in the air in victory.

"They got 'im. Apparently, the motorboat wouldn't start."

The occupants of the room sat down to recover from the climax, trying to make sense of the events to which they had participated and witnessed.

Fifteen minutes later, Jennifer and Bevyn watched the Bakerstreet staff and guests, as well as the police officers, file out of the room. Olivia came over to the professor and congratulated him in her singsong voice.

"Why, Bevyn, looks like we need extra help around here now. We could use an able-bodied man like you."

"I'm sure you can find a replacement."

She tilted her head in the demure fashion women use when not willing to impose their charms on a man and brought her hand up to Bevyn. He kissed it. Gervais came over, and they watched Olivia float out of the room. He thanked Bevyn and apologized for his error earlier in the evening. Bevyn extended his hand. They shook, and Gervais left to attend to his men.

Murphy approached. "I have to hand it to you, there, Sherlock. It was a tough one."

"Caroline seemed almost too helpful, and having the black dress was a good catalyst, but I wasn't sure about the blackmail. Just a hunch."

"Bevyn, I don't understand. Where the dress came from?"

"Courtesy of the Bakerstreet Mystery Retreat costume department."

"We never found the original," Murphy added with a devious grin.

Bevyn leaned back on his heels and bounced. "A little sleight-of-hand to catch a killer," Bevyn sighed. "The star in all this was Beth. She really was the catalyst for me to persist." Bevyn's voice was tinged with sorrow.

The chief scratched his bald spot and stuck a finger in one of his suspenders. He paused when he saw that Jennifer was about to speak. She smiled, but her face went serious. "Who terrorized the actor?"

"Let me guess, Bevyn. Probably Mack?" Murphy speculated.

"Probably. I wouldn't put it past him. I am sure he scared the hell out of him. Wasn't coming out of retirement worth it, Chief?"

Murphy screwed up his eyes and gave the comment mock serious thought before shaking his head. "It was all worth it. Poor

Beth to get mixed up in this whole mess. Bob probably tried to seduce her back at his place, and she refused, giving him more reason to see her dead." He gave Jennifer a side hug. "I'm sorry for you and your friend."

Jennifer made a sound with her mouth. "I guess people can't escape the past, sometimes. Sad."

"She'll probably get a lighter sentence considering her past abuse at the hand of Peters."

"I know people who suffered as much or more than she did, and they don't go around having people whacked," Murphy remarked.

"But aren't we all capable given extreme circumstance?"

Jennifer and Chief Murphy paused to consider Bevyn's rhetorical question. The police detective's eyes grew large. "What about the note?"

"I don't think there was one," Murphy muttered and added, "Mack sure caused a lot of havoc around here."

Bevyn tipped his hat. "Including scaring me with the crossbow and then trying to drown me with Bob's other gorilla."

Jennifer cleared her voice. "I think Clint was the real fool in all this."

Murphy nodded. "We got Bob on offshore gambling, along with Shawna and company. Clint'll probably rat out Caroline and vice versa over the blackmail. She found out about Bob's operation, from all her poking around, and blackmailed him to kill Beth. So Bob wanted her dead as extra insurance."

"So, she wasn't lying about the threats, Bevyn?" Jennifer said.

"No, she had a bull's eye on her back."

Jennifer suddenly excused herself and went to talk to the CO who was about to leave the room. The two men stood in silence, contemplating the events of the evening.

"I'll take your input on Mrs. Samuels. She's an old woman I think you'll agree . . ."

Bevyn flipped the toonie that he removed from his pocket. "I don't think she knew what she was doing. If my daughter had been touched by that dirty old man Peters, I might have done the same thing."

Murphy nodded and exhaled his breath. "Well, that's one

cold case off the books."

"Did they ever suspect her?"

Murphy played with his cell phone. "Hard to say, but they had no motive to work with." Murphy levelled a gaze at Bevyn. "It goes against my better judgment . . ."

"I'm sure whatever happened in that boathouse long ago will remain there. It could have been an accident like she says—a few heated words, jostling. What would you have done if you found out your daughter had been molested?" Bevyn pontificated philosophically. "Sometimes, it's better to serve justice rather than the law."

Murphy made a clicking sound with his tongue. He lowered his voice. "The inheritance didn't go to the son; it went to Peters' brother."

Bevyn nodded. "It figures. He's wanted to confess something to me. I feel it."

He studied the interaction between the CO and Detective Watson. Murphy poked the professor in the arm. "She's a fine woman and detective."

The professor examined a coin he had removed from his trouser pocket and adjusted his shoulders. "She's the kind of woman worth waiting for."

Murphy chuckled. "I wouldn't wait too long." He caught Bevyn's eye. "What's next?"

Bevyn gazed into the distance, a crooked smiled spreading across his face touched with a trace of grimness. "We celebrate, and tomorrow I have to take a difficult little trip to the monastery to clear up the past."

Chapter XVIII

Geese flew high in the sky, honking on the route south for the winter, and a layer of heavy frost covered the trees and ground. Winter threatened to take an early grip on the land as it had many times before, but readers of the *Farmer's Almanac* disagreed. Grey clouds hung low on the horizon like portents of the events about to unfold. By the time Bevyn reached the monastery, overnight frost had begun to melt under the warmth of the sun's rays.

The monks had just finished matins. The *portière*, Brother Jean, and Bevyn chatted briefly about the closing of the Oka monastery near Montreal.

"It's the end of a tradition. Where will we go to contemplate in our 24/7 world?"

"In our living rooms in front of screens," Bevyn replied, half-joking and half-serious.

The Frenchman brought the tips of his hands to his chin in the shape of a steeple. *"Peut-être, peut-être."* He remained unconvinced despite the professor's words of encouragement.

Bevyn bid the old man farewell and went looking for

Brother Kirk. He found the English monk in the sanctuary, gazing at the organ pipes in the altar area. He pumped the detective's hand and guessed the reason for the visit.

"A dying man can't get far," Kirk exclaimed.

Bevyn tweaked his shoulders. "You'd be surprised." He winked.

"Ah, yes, quite. It's amazing that a carpenter could impact the world so much."

"He remained true to the end. I cannot say the same," Bevyn responded.

The old monk brought his hands together in derision. "When you learn to see as a child again, you'll find your way."

"Perhaps. I just lost my way somewhere. But we digress. I expected that Peters is in his quarters resting?"

Kirk struck the pose of a violinist playing a melodic passage. "No doubt he is in the music hall listening to a piano and violin recital."

They sat down in the front pew and watched three brothers prepare the altar for late morning mass. For some time, the two men sat in silence. One of the monks cleaning the altar recognized Bevyn and grasped his arm in affection. He traded a few pleasantries with Bevyn and then left with the other two monks.

A twinge of regret pulsed through Bevyn's body as he watched them go. He had taken a fork in the road. Never one to second guess, he found himself at another crossroads in his life. Kirk glanced over at his companion. Bevyn let out a quick sigh.

"Certainty is not the mark of a courageous life. We choose as best as we can," Kirk counselled.

The door at the back of the sanctuary opened. Two familiar voices began a brief, heated conversation. It ended, and Bevyn heard the sound of a cart coming their way.

"Brother Kirk and Master Bevyn, I apologize for not being here sooner, but I needed to be accosted by the dom apparently."

Brother Peters sat in the pew with them. The three men were alone in the sanctuary.

"I know what brings you here, Bevyn."

Bevyn smiled at the dying monk.

"Maybe I should be going," Brother Kirk exclaimed, preparing to leave.

Bevyn touched Kirk's arm. "No, you are here for a reason, if it's all right with you." Bevyn looked at Peters for agreement.

The old monk nodded. A spasm racked his body. He reached into his habit and produced a pill that he swallowed. A wan smile crossed his lips.

Bevyn stared at the ceiling of the sanctuary where the sun hit the rafters. The precision of the post and beam construction held his fascination. He curled and uncurled the fingers on his left hand. With a deep breath, he brought his eyes to the old monk's. "I need to know the truth about your brother."

The old man's face went blank. He didn't reply for a while and then slowly wagged his head as though he had Parkinson's. "Bevyn, we shared honour and integrity," he managed to say while spittle collected in one corner of his mouth and the remains of scrambled eggs rested on his upper lip.

"You taught me about integrity being the basis for *life*, not just the dojo!"

"Bevyn, how can I make you understand?"

Bevyn stepped onto the marble altar and ran his hand along the polished brass rail. A wooden carving of Christ on the cross captured his attention for its detail, down to the crown of thorns on Jesus' head. His voice echoed in the nave. "Why?"

"I think you know. We all start this life with noble ambitions and then we forget about what matters. It's not complicated. But I have set things right."

The feelings in his heart for the old monk conflicted with his distaste for unnecessary human suffering. The reality of historical facts dulled his conscience. They were impersonal, forgivable, understandable, but a stronger force spoke from deep inside his soul.

The old sensei added to his confession in an impartial tone of voice. "My brother was not a good man. He had a history of molesting girls. The family knew about it and did nothing."

Kirk pointed a crooked finger in Peters' face, and the monk bowed his head. What does that have to do with why we're here?"

"Do you know how difficult truth is? Lawsuits, chaos, families falling apart. We're always choosing the lesser evil in this life when we vote, when we marry, when we carry out our mission, when we . . ." Brother Peters began to cough. It racked his body and persisted for an alarming amount of time, doubling the old man over in pain.

Bevyn stepped closer to his old sensei, his face grim. "We must get him to his room. I fear there is not much time now."

"His conscience condemns him," Kirk muttered with little mercy.

They half-dragged, half-carried Peters back to the infirmary. The attendant took one look at Peters and indicated for Kirk and Bevyn to bring him to his room. He admonished them and went to call the physician. Bevyn looked at his sensei, his surrogate father, a man who played a role in his life where there had been no one to any depth or degree—just an impatient uncle and a grandfather who preferred to remain reticent about life. And now, his father-figure lay near death, wanting to take secrets with him. Bevyn wondered if he had the right to extract a confession, to get the old man to admit to doing nothing to protect another life.

Peters' doctor arrived in record time out of breath and carrying a medical bag. After a few minutes, he came out, face downcast, speaking low. Bevyn asked if he could speak to the patient. The doctor shrugged and announced softly that the old man's death was imminent.

Bevyn entered the room. The old sensei lay on his back, his watery eyes staring at the ceiling. He lifted his hand and indicated for his protégé to take it. With a heavy heart, the student grasped the teacher's skeletal limb. "You were like a son I never had . . ." Peters said in a raspy voice.

He closed his eyes and groaned. His tongue sought teeth that were no longer in his mouth. He pointed to the ceiling with a finger. "There are about 2,000 thousand squares on the ceiling. Ironic, no? Two thousand years since the Christ. I have counted them many times these last few weeks, yes, many times."

A hacking fit consumed him. His face went to a shade of grey that alarmed Bevyn. He released his grasp on the old monk's hand to get the doctor, but Peters held on tighter. The doctor rushed in and went to Peters's side.

"I see Him and all the angels, Master Bevyn. I kept my word."

Bevyn searched the man's eyes, looking for some kind of absolution until he pictured in his mind's eye a small alcove in the lower bowels of the church where a man and a boy met to learn about Christ, martial arts, life, and prayer.

Bevyn gave his final farewells, conflicted but aware a confession in the traditional sense would not be forthcoming.

Peters' eyes blinked a few times, his face went slack, and then Bevyn felt Peters' hand go limp. The doctor shook his head. Kirk appeared at the door.

Bevyn and Kirk recited a prayer for the dead as the doctor looked on. The attendant entered the room and spoke with the monastery physician. Bevyn and Kirk left, their hands clasped behind their backs. They reached the end of the hall and stood before a window that gave a panoramic view of the lake. After a few moments, Kirk broke the silence.

"The monastery doorman told me he saw Peters talking to Brent a few days ago. I forgot to tell you. It must've slipped my mind."

Bevyn prodded the old monk for more details.

"The dom interrupted the conversation and sent Brent on a wild goose chase to Bakerstreet with a cockeyed story about a treasure being hidden there years ago."

"Sounds like something Chevalier would do. Hard to believe Brent and Ivan believed him," Bevyn said.

"What did Peters mean when he said he set things right?"

"The inheritance money from his brother went to build a network of shelters for abused women."

Kirk fiddled with his habit as silence fell between them. After some moments, Kirk proposed a game plan. "We could pump Chevalier for more details, but something tells me you are not going to do that."

Bevyn glanced over his shoulder at Peters' room and twirled a few strands of hair at the nape of his neck. He switched his gaze to the orchard below, the trees aligned like tombstones. "I don't think it's relevant to the matter at the boathouse and I'm not a treasure hunter."

Kirk nodded his head as he considered Bevyn's admission. He wanted to know more about The Secret and the clues in the pictures. It would be a fine challenge for his restless mind. He returned to the present.

"What next, professor?" Kirk said.

Bevyn stroked his wrist before answering. "We live with the certainty of uncertainty and try not to second guess ourselves."

Kirk raised a hand for Bevyn to wait. Bevyn watched the actor rack his brains, trying to remember something. Kirk stroked his chin, clapped his hands, and smacked his lips. Then he quoted from Hamlet.

"And, like a man to double business bound, I stand in pause where I shall first begin, and both neglect."

Bevyn chuckled, put an arm around Kirk, and gave his own version of the quote in Latin.

"Dum deliberamus quando incipiendum, incipere jam serum fit."

Kirk considered the speech for a moment and then nodded his head. He ventured a guess as to the Latin author's providence and the English translation of the quote. "Cicero. 'When we consider where to begin, it becomes too late to do so.'"

"Yes," Bevyn smiled ruefully. "But it's Quintilian."

Kirk joined Bevyn's side, and they gazed at the sun slipping behind the small mountain surrounding the lake. Orange streaks of sunlight shot across the lake's tranquil surface. A few minutes later, the orange orb vanished, leaving the great Eastern Township's granite sky in its wake—a solemn reminder of human folly and the brevity of human existence on earth.

Acknowledgments

Many people have been involved directly or indirectly in the writing of this book.

In chronological order, I owe the following people a tremendous amount of gratitude. First, to my teachers who saw early promise: Mrs. Maclean in elementary school; Mr. Ward in high school, where I published a short prose piece in the Galt yearbook; Prof. Rudy Nassar at Champlain College, Lennoxville, who gave me the freedom to write for the college newspaper, *The Champlain Review*; Dr. Jan Draper who inspired me beyond words to write and create—so much so, she became my unofficial mentor; and Anne Diamond (Maclean) and Colin Browne of the Department of Creative Writing at Concordia University.

I extend further gratitude to Arthur Miriello, a spiritual brother and a great historical fiction writer; Christian Roy for his enthusiasm about the project; Andrew Calder who said once, "David, write until beads of blood drip onto the page"; and Mr. Russ Bailey for his gift as a storyteller and someone who believed in me.

Lastly, thanks to my mother who encouraged her kids to read and who read the early manuscripts and my blog. To my sisters, Cheryl and Dyan, love you lots for putting up with my big imagination all these years! I would like to extend a final thanks to *"ma tante Mai"* for showing me unconditional love.

Montreal, 2013

Manufactured by Amazon.ca
Bolton, ON